Praise for THE WILD BLUE YONDER

"The wild blue yonder, the laughter and the pain: these are the chosen territories of Audrey Thomas. She navigates them with uncommon skill and bold instincts."

Books in Canada

"Audrey Thomas is one of this country's most skilled prose scrutinizers of the current state of play between the sexes."

Kingston Whig-Standard

"Ms. Thomas is...closely acquainted with the mysterious territory of the human heart and details her characters' emotional struggles with humor and compassion."

Winnipeg Free Press

"Canada's best anatomist of male-female relationships."

Edmonton Journal

"She uses the places and people she has known—and she has lived adventurously—with great skill. She can write as confidently through the eyes of a nine-year-old boy as through those of a middle-aged woman."

Toronto Star

"These characters and their dilemmas, crafted with Thomas's fine command of literary devices and masterful use of language, make for a stirring collection of stories."

Victoria Times-Colonist

"Thomas has an unerring fix on human pain and joy and she tells her stories with skill and insight."

Toronto Sun

"A masterful combination of compression and precision."

Montreal Gazette

"What...[Audrey Thomas] is doing in this collection of stories is displaying the power of a writer working at the top of her form."

The Globe and Mail

PENGUIN BOOKS

The Wild Blue Yonder

Audrey Thomas was born and raised in New York State but has lived and worked on Canada's west coast since 1959. Her other short story collections include *Two in the Bush and Other Stories*, *Real Mothers* and *Goodbye Harold, Good Luck*. She is also the author of a number of highly acclaimed novels, including *Latakia*, *Mrs. Blood*, *Songs my Mother Taught Me* and *Intertidal Life*, which was nominated for a Governor General's Award and won the B.C. Book Prize. She has written over fifteen radio plays and been nominated for an ACTRA Award. Audrey Thomas has taught at many of Canada's universities and is the recipient of the Canada-Scotland Writer's Literary Fellowship as well as many other awards and distinctions. She lives on Galiano Island, B.C., where she is working on her next novel.

THE
WILD BLUE
YONDER

Audrey Thomas

Penguin Books

PENGUIN BOOKS
Published by the Penguin Group
Penguin Books Canada Ltd, 10 Alcorn Avenue, Toronto, Ontario,
Canada M4V 3B2
Penguin Books Ltd, 27 Wrights Lane, London W8 5TZ, England
Penguin Books USA Inc., 375 Hudson Street, New York,
New York 10014, U.S.A.
Penguin Books Australia Ltd, Ringwood, Victoria, Australia
Penguin Books (NZ) Ltd, 182-190 Wairau Road,
Auckland 10, New Zealand

Penguin Books Ltd, Registered Offices: Harmondsworth,
Middlesex, England

First published in Viking by Penguin Books Canada Limited, 1990

Published in Penguin Books, 1991

1 3 5 7 9 10 8 6 4 2

Copyright © Audrey Thomas, 1990
All rights reserved

*Publisher's note: This book is a work of fiction. Names, characters, places and
incidents either are the product of the author's imagination or are used
fictitiously, and any resemblance to actual persons living or dead, events, or
locales is entirely coincidental.*

Manufactured in Canada

"Compression" first appeared in *The Moosehead Anthology*;
"Breeders" first appeared in *The Capilano Review*;
"A Hunter's Moon" first appeared in *The Malahat Review.*

Canadian Cataloguing in Publication Data

Thomas, Audrey, 1935-
The wild blue yonder

ISBN 0-14-012604-X

I. Title.

PS8539.H64W5   1991   C813'.54   C90-094163-4
PR9199.3.T45W5   1991

American Library of Congress Cataloguing in
Publication Data Available

*To my Concordia students
without whose enthusiasm for the short story,
there might have been two more stories in my book.*

THE
WILD BLUE
YONDER

Contents

Roots

Roots

"Now I understand about smithereens," Louise said. The teapot lay in pieces on the kitchen floor. "There's an interesting word," her husband said, getting up from the table. "Irish, I'll bet. I'll just go look it up." His ears stood out from his head, as did the ears of his sons. Because of who he was (a radio sound technician and a lover of words) she always saw his ears as some sort of catcher's mitt, plucking out of the air whatever new and exciting word was hurled his way. Nine years ago she had thought it was charming; now it drove her nuts.

"And poor Earl Grey," he said, "a soggy mess. Never mind, there's more of him in the cupboard." But she did mind. There he was, off to his dictionaries while she got paper towels and the dustpan. The teapot, a Brown Betty, was the first present he had ever given her. It had survived several moves and a trip across the ocean. She hadn't been paying attention — it was her own fault the teapot broke, but that didn't make it any better. She'd been thinking about the new neighbour and how she always, always, always had to deal with the real world while Michael went around with his head in the clouds.

Yesterday the neighbour, a short, fat, fussy man in his sixties had come over to complain about the dandelions. If they weren't mowed down soon, they would turn white and the dandelion seeds would travel next door and along the street. Kevin and Alexander had stopped riding their tricycle and junior bike and come to listen. Now Kevin interrupted. "Did you know they're called dandelions because their leaves look like lion's teeth? Did you know that? Here, I'll show you." He picked one (one of dozens that dotted the lawn) and brought it over. Alexander, who copied what he could of everything his older brother said and did, grabbed some yellow heads. "Lion," he said to the neighbour, "grrr, grrr." The neighbour was not amused.

Louise was about to remind Michael about the lawn, which had remained half-mowed for weeks, when her elbow knocked the teapot off the counter. And here he was now, coming down the stairs all smiles, with a dictionary in his hand.

"Just as I thought," he said, "Anglo-Irish, from smithers, 'small pieces or fragments, ultimately from smith.' But dictionaries don't always tell the truth. Maybe, like the Hooligans, they were an Irish family, small people (from years of intermarriage and god knows what kind of incestuous slap and tickle going on) — sort of a cross between leprechauns and munchkins. They lived on a farm in Kerry and begat nothing but daughters. Three daughters — as in all the best tales it had to be three — named Eileen, Maureen and Kathleen. Three lovely colleens from Kerry. They were highly emotional girls, as was their mother. They keened a lot, at weddings, at funerals, at births, the phases of the moon, the price of two yards of ribbon for their petticoats. When they appeared in the nearest village the villagers would shout, 'Here come the wailing women,' and lock their doors. For when they got really worked up they threw things, smashed them into small pieces which came to be called smithereens. It was because of this smashing habit that the girls, in spite of their great beauty, remained unmarried until their dying day.''

''Oh,'' he said, ''oh don't!'' He took the last two steps in a leap, the dictionary tumbling to the floor. She was standing there holding the yellow dustpan and sobbing. There was a bright spot of blood on the tip of her nose where she had pricked herself while bent down and searching for the last fragments. ''Oh love, don't,'' he said, holding her tight, ''I'll buy you another.'' He tilted her head back and licked her nose with his tongue. ''You've pricked your nose.'' ''Have I?'' she said bitterly, drawing away. ''Have I pricked myself and no prince came? Just not my lucky day.'' She knew she had wounded him but was beyond caring.

His voice shook a little. ''No, no prince. Whoever heard of a prince with a bald spot on the top of his head? Princes have luxuriant heads of hair, always, which they wear in an attractive pageboy bob.'' ''I'm sorry,'' she said, and she was. ''But you drove me to it. Whoever heard of a princess with stretch marks?''

He had been right there when the boys were born, rubbing her back, encouraging her. She'd hated him then as well. ''Why are there men!'' she yelled, when Kevin's head broke through the ring of fire that was her vagina, her ''birth canal'' as the nurse had called it during prenatal classes. Canal had sounded cool and green, but there had been nothing cool or orderly about that birth or the next one. Afterwards, she felt as though she were straddling a barbed-wire fence. Both children were born face up.

''I think his ears got caught,'' he said that first night. ''Next time choose a man with a pinhead and ears like cockleshells, and you'll do better. Mothers should tell their daughters that; never mind income or colour of his eyes. Measure his head before you make any commitments.''

But the pain was soon forgotten and the love remained. ''Listen,'' she said now, leading him over to the table and sitting down. ''Maybe I'm just getting old or something, but I can't take it any more. And I'm ashamed of that fact: I feel I've failed because these days your silliness drives me crazy. Oh, I know, as an article in one of those women's magazines we'd go over big. ''Cheerful disorder,'' they'd say. ''Comfortably shabby,'' they'd call this place — or I'd say it, so they'd know I like it the way it is. And you'd be the loving, playful, imaginative father who reads poetry to his sons every night and teaches them that the word 'salary' comes from salt, and why, and the word 'tulip' comes from an Eastern turban. Who enriches their childhood world with his love of words.'' He opened his mouth to speak, but she held up her hand. ''Let me finish. Meanwhile, meanwhile, while all this enrichment is going on the lawn remains half-mowed and the lawnmower rusts because you and the boys are off on some adventure. And the neighbour complains to me, not to you, about the dandelions. As though I were responsible.''

''You could have finished the lawn.''

''You said you'd do it, therefore it's your job.''

He stood up shouting ''Oh job blob gob slob fob/ oh *fuck* the new neighbour. What is the matter with you?'' Louise looked down at the placemat and not at him. It was a copy of an old nineteenth-century label. Her sister had sent them a set for Christmas last year. This one was of an enormous red tomato. Wayne County Preserving Co. was printed below. The tomato mocked her with its healthy red perfection.

''I don't know, Michael. But I just don't find it enchanting any more, that you treat life as a game.''

''I take life very seriously.'' He sat down again.

''No you don't.''

''Indeed I do. It's far more important to take the boys

to see the dinosaur exhibit than it is to finish the lawn. I want to awaken all their senses. I want to teach them to think. You used to come on our 'adventures' as well, remember?''

"You know what I think? I think you want to be the perfect father, that's what I think. Some kind of over-compensation maybe, who knows.'' Oh how could she have said such a terrible thing! She reached for him but he stood up again. His face was white.

"Forgive me for ending this interesting conversation, but duty calls. I must arise now and go to mow the lawn. Honour thy neighbour or something like that.'' He left the house calling for the boys to get the rake.

The kitchen window was open. "Dad, why was Mum cryin', Dad?'' "She broke something special. Remember when you broke your new kite. You cried really hard?'' "But why are you cryin', Dad?'' Louise put her hands over her ears.

Louise met Michael in a pub in London, England. He had come up to her and her girlfriend and while waiting for his pint (the place was very crowded) he asked, in a broad Texas drawl, if London was always so dark and rainy. When they answered with North American accents he seemed taken aback for a minute and then grinned and continued. You didn't notice his ears at first; you noticed the grin and the dark curly hair. "Ah guess ah read too much Wordsworth at school,'' he said, accepting his drink from the barmaid and squeezing onto the banquette where they were sitting. "Ah thought spring would be full of daffodils and sunshine. That fellow Browning misled me as well. Perhaps it was all part of an early public-relations plot, like Greenland or the Cape of Good Hope. Where you-all from?''

He relaxed when they said they were Canadians on holiday from their au pair jobs in Toulouse. Maybe he just didn't want to meet fellow Americans. "London's really very nice," Louise said, "even in the rain. Galleries and movies and bookshops and plays. Or maybe you don't like any of those things?" There was definitely something strange about him, the intent look as well as the ears, which she now noticed, sitting as she was, only inches away from him. He was attractive nevertheless. She'd never met a Texan before; maybe that was it.

"Ah've been spendin' a lot of my time (mah tie-um) in the British Museum Readin' Room," he said. "Ah'm doin' a dissertation on Dickens. He lived right around here for a while, on Doughty Street. This here is supposed to have been his favourite pub. That's why Ah came in." He paused. "And because Ah was so darned bored and lonely and tired of walkin' around in the rain." His curly hair was just beginning to dry out. Stuck to his head like that, it reminded Louise of the chiselled hair on Greek and Roman statues. However, it made his ears even more noticeable than they might otherwise have been. "Ah see you-all are fascinated by mah ears." "Oh no, no. Really." Was her face as red as Deborah's? "Oh yes, yes, really. Well mah mother did her best. She stuck them back against mah head every night with stickin' plaster; she turned me to one side and then the other every night of my infant life, but it didn't do any good." He smiled at her anxiously. "Do you think my children would be affected? I mean, mah Daddy and Granddaddy had ears like this. Do you think it would be fair to bring more of us into the world? Ah mean, would you marry a man whose ears stood out like this?" "Of course." He grabbed her hand. "Good, then we're engaged. How long will you be in town?"

The bartender called time and the stranger let go of her hand. He stood up as they gathered their coats and bags. "I've got a confession to make," he said in a very English voice. "I'm not a Texan at all. I was so relieved when you two said you were Canadians. Tell me, did I fool you?"

"Not for a minute," Louise said and headed for the door. "Come on Deborah. It's been nice meeting you, whoever you are. I hope you won your bet." She was furious. To have been taken in like that! No doubt he and his buddies would have a big laugh about it later. He followed them out of the pub. "Good-night Michael," the barmaid called. "Look," he said, "don't be angry. It wasn't a bet, except with myself maybe. I'm an actor and at 10 A.M. tomorrow I have to audition for a part in a Sam Shepard play. I'd been practising all day, and seeing you two in the pub, hearing you when you ordered, well I thought you were Americans. So I took the plunge." He said all this to their backs, following them to the end of the street.

"Right!" he suddenly shouted, "look right!" He yanked them back on the curb. "Oh Lord," he said as they stood there in the rain. "Think how I'd feel if you two got knocked down because you were mad at me. Please, forgive me. May I take you both to dinner tomorrow night? If I get the part we might even have a bottle of wine. If I don't we can have beer."

"Did I really fool you?" he asked, as he left them at the door of their Bed and Breakfast. They assured him he had, but they were only Canadians after all. "I've never even met a Texan," Louise said. "You sounded like a television Texan at any rate," Deborah said. "My French family watches 'Dallas.' " He disappeared into the rain and mist. *Merde!* They called after him, "Break a leg!"

He — Michael — didn't get the part and Louise bought the wine. He took her to a pizza parlour where a string quartet played Mozart. Deborah decided not to come along. "It's you he's after." "Don't be silly. Anyway, we're leaving tomorrow." "We're only going across the Channel." "Don't be such a romantic!" "Tell me one thing," Deborah said, "would you really marry a man whose ears stuck out like that?" "I can't see what ears have to do with it?'' ''Good. Well then, honeychile Ah'm goin' ta that new art movie in Brunswick Square. You can tell me all about your evening when you come in.''

The dictionary was still sprawled on the bottom step. Mare to Z and Addenda. All sorts of things had fallen out because he marked places in books with whatever was to hand! Popsicle sticks, shoelaces, envelopes, colour strips for paint, dollar bills. It occurred to her now that he must care deeply to throw down one of his beloved dictionaries. She picked it up, intending to put it back upstairs but the book fell open to a page where a red rose had been carefully taped in. Louise sat on the bottom step and began to read.

''It doesn't really matter all that much about the part,'' he said that night in the pizza parlour, ''except for money — the lack of it, of course. My ego isn't shattered is what I mean. My real love is radio. Why on radio a blind man can play a World War II flying ace. If he should care to do so, a one-legged man can tap dance, a fellow with jug-ears and the right voice can play the romantic lead. It's the most democratic place imaginable. I love it. I'd far rather work in radio than on the stage. But I'll always be grateful to Sam Shepard — I might even sit down tonight and pen him a thank-you letter.'' ''Why's that?'' ''Because he led me to you. Gave me both an excuse and the courage to talk to you. Now I wonder if you'll let me write to you, maybe even come to Toulouse for a visit?'' Which he did, after several letters. Charming Louise's ''family'' with his terrible French and bearing flowers for Maman. A brown teapot for Louise. In the kitchen that night, the children in bed and Maman and Papa gone to their country house for the weekend, Michael insisted on making a pot of good English tea. ''I can do it.'' ''No, no. You've put the little monsters to bed, I'll do it. Besides, you're a Canadian, it isn't the same if a Canadian makes it. I mean, do you always take the pot to the kettle? Do you?'' From one of his pockets he produced a tea-ball already filled with tea. ''I was a Scout,'' he said, ''you know our motto.''

As they sat at the kitchen table, waiting for the tea to steep, he said, ''Canada or Australia, what do you think? I'd say Canada myself, Australians always seem to be somewhere else sending postcards home. The girls I meet — the Australian girls (her heart gave a little lurch) — don't just go away on holiday for a month or two, they go for years. Doesn't that tell you something about Australia? Their slang might be fun to study however. Here he did an imitation of a jackaroo. ''Have you already had enough of Canada or would you be interested in returning there?'' ''I am returning there. In exactly two months and seven days. I'm travelling for a month with Deborah and then we have to go home and get ready to go back to school.'' Louise was intent on getting a degree in early-childhood education.

He poured out the tea, frowned at the teapot and held it up to his ear. ''I think there's something funny about this teapot.'' ''What?'' ''I'm not sure.'' From another pocket he produced a bag of sweet biscuits. ''Is that a fixed ticket. I mean, can you change it?'' ''Why would I do that?'' They looked at one another. ''These biscuits,'' she said, ''are called *'les langues de chat.'* Cat's tongues. Or did you already know that?'' ''I just pointed.'' ''Liar.'' He drank all his tea in three swallows.

''God I'm thirsty. It must be all that garlic in the soup. You know, when somebody takes a leave without permission we say in England that they take 'French leave.' The French say, 'To take English leave.' There's a lot of animosity between the French and English. Funny, I like the French. Especially their language. Hey, think about that word, language. And these biscuits, these *'langues.'* I'd never really thought of that before, about language and tongue. Of course, we say our 'mother tongue' is such and such, but we say it without thinking." He was talking faster and faster, holding the teapot up to his ear and shaking it. Finally, he went and poured the rest of the tea into the sink. Then he pulled out the tea-caddy and presented it to her. "I think this is the problem," he said, setting it before her on a tea-towel. "What d'you mean?" "Open it," he said. "Don't burn your fingers." In the midst of the wet tea-leaves was an old-fashioned Victorian ring with a tiny garnet in its centre. "You're an idiot," Louise said, blinking away the tears, "you hardly know me." "You don't know me at all," he said, suddenly really serious. "Remember all that palaver about my daddy and granddaddy's ears in the Lamb that night? Well, I have no idea what my granddaddy's ears looked like, or my daddy's, or any other part of him for that matter. I'm an orphan, Louise. Were I a word, the Oxford English Dictionary would put o.o.o. after me!" "Of obscure origin." "Other dictionaries might put etym. dub. I am eternally grateful to my adoptive parents, who live just outside Liverpool. I hope you will come with me to meet them. Can you imagine anyone choosing a jug-eared baby and taking him home? I am eternally grateful to them for that, but they aren't exactly affectionate people, my mother and father. They made sure I had good health and a good education and that I didn't end up talking with a Merseyside accent. I teased them about that later on, after the Beatles. Just think, I could have had every girl in England hanging on my words!" "How would they feel about your leaving England?" "They might be a bit sad, but they would feel I was doing the right thing. I would come back and visit, of course. And they could come out. They aren't rich, but they aren't poor either. My dad's retired now but he used to be Chief Accountant with the Midland Bank. But that's not important. What is important, Louise, is that there may be stranger things in my genetic background than big ears.

Would that worry you?'' ''No,'' she said. ''I don't think so. But don't your adopted parents know anything at all?'' ''Nothing. I was found screaming my head off in the ladies' cloakroom of a department store. Very early one morning. I had probably been there overnight.'' He smiled painfully. ''Liverpool is — was — a big port. No doubt, my father was a sailor. Or one of the Irish who came over to find work on the docks. I keep thinking I'll see him someday — I have a feeling I'd hardly fail to recognize him.'' He smiled painfully. ''Did you know that 'to abandon' means 'to set free'?'' he asked. (Louise could hear her parents . . . ''But his background darling? What are his roots?'')

''Michael,'' Louise said, ''will you marry me? I should tell you right now that I want children. More than one, anyway. Two or three.''

The lawn was mowed and the mower put away, but Michael and the boys were nowhere around. They had probably gone downtown to buy her a new teapot. Or maybe not. What she had said was unforgiveable. She decided to have him paged at all the department stores she could think of but he wasn't there — not at any of them. She tried the Provincial Museum. Not there either. Words were such powerful things. Sometimes they were like dangerous animals — once let out there was no telling the damage they could do. She grabbed her jacket and decided to go in search of her family.

And she found them in the park, at the petting zoo. Michael was taking a picture of a young Japanese couple. The girl was very pretty. Kevin took his mother's hand, just as if it were the most natural thing in the world that she should rush up at that moment, wild-haired and red in the face from running. ''They're on their animal,'' Kevin said, ''that's why Dad's taking their picture.'' ''Animoo,'' said Alexander. The girl giggled and called to Louise, ''Yes, yes, on our animoo.'' ''Honeymoon,''

Michael said, "you're on your honeymoon." "Yes, yes," the girl said, laughing, "hanimoo"

After the picture had been taken and introductions made, the Japanese girl explained that she taught "baby school." She knelt in the grass in her beautiful red wool suit, and sang them a nursery song in Japanese. "I was wondering," Michael said, "if you'd like to invite the Tanabes back for tea?" He held up a square box with a Union Jack on the side. "What did the song say?" Kevin asked. Louise looked at him. "Does it matter?"

The Japanese girl was rummaging through her shopping bags. "We too!" she said. And held up a square box with a Union Jack on the side. "Genuine alicah," her husband said.

They stood there, holding their teapots, smiling at one another. What will my sons remember, Louise thinks, years from now? The new black lamb, the pretty Japanese woman in her red suit, the dandelions? Or their father and mother shouting about a teapot broken on the kitchen floor.

The Slow
of Despond

The Slow
of Despond

Once a year, on a certain day in November, Sarah MacLeod put on her wedding ring and paid a visit to the Palm Houses in Edinburgh's Royal Botanic Gardens. She had done this for more than twenty-five years and yet, each time, her hand felt strange with the ring upon it, hot and heavy under the sheepskin glove. This year she had set out a bit later than usual, so she hurried a little as she crossed to Inverleith Row towards the East Entrance. It was already half past two and the gardens closed an hour before sunset.

(She was never able to resist glancing at the papers before she even left the newsagents, not *The Guardian* or *The Independent*, which she saved for later, but the local paper, *The Scotsman*. It was on the third page, just a small item but it leapt out at her like a cat. It sprang. "Reverend Gordon MacLeod and his wife." "Illustrated talk on Zambia." Then the time and the place. Zambia! So that's where he had ended up. The Rev. Gordon MacLeod and his wife. "Mrs MacLeod?" The newsagent's wife called to her over the shelves of magazines and sweets. "Are you all right?")

The afternoon was beautiful, cold but clear and cloudless, with no wind and the gardens were full of toddlers running along the paths, young mothers pushing prams and old people sitting on benches, their faces turned up towards the sun. She smiled at a mother teaching her daughter a song Sarah had known long ago.

"Peter Pointer, Peter Pointer, where are you?" sang the mother, shaking the child's index finger gently up and down. "Here I am, here I am, how do you do." Sometimes Sarah brought along the little boy from across the stair — Eric. He called the Palm Houses "the hot trees."

The next would be Tommy Tall, then Ruby Ring, Ruby Ring, but what was the little finger called? She couldn't remember. The hands of the child, chubby, dimpled, reminded Sarah of animal crackers. The little girl had red hair and freckles and would be about three and a half. The Scottish children were so beautiful — so bonny — until they grew up and started stuffing themselves with takeaway food and pastries. Even Eric's mother, Sheena, was already heavy and pale at twenty-three. Sarah had never got used to the monotony of the vegetables, potatoes and swedes, potatoes and carrots and swedes and the sky-high price of anything else. Yesterday, she had paid 68p for a small head of broccoli. Other things were available of course, but so expensive they were looked upon as treats. It was no wonder people filled up on chips or those dreadful pizzas whose round styrofoam covers littered the streets on weekends. They looked like abandoned toilet seats.

Sarah had never seen so many red-headed people as there were in Edinburgh, all shades from the palest copper of a new penny through deep chestnut. There were even red-haired mannequins in some of the department-store windows along Princes Street. Her own hair had darkened almost to brown but when she had first come to Scotland she had fit right in, in terms of colouring, and her passport still listed her hair as "auburn," a small vanity she found hard to give up.

Who came after Ruby Ring? It bothered her that she couldn't remember.

She moved off the path and onto the grass to go round a place where a group of gardeners — one of them a young woman — were topping some trees.

DANGEROUS TREE WORK said a sign across the path. CAUTION. The British were fond of signs, always politely put of course. Any excuse would do: CAUTION, MIND YOUR HEAD, QUEUE THIS SIDE. This sign should be in Latin, in keeping with all the other signs in the main gardens. It was the one thing that annoyed her here: all the tags on the trees and shrubs and flowers were in Latin and although she could make out a few words here and there she had never enjoyed Latin in high school and had dropped it after her second year. Surely very few of the ordinary people who enjoyed these gardens could translate the tags? But perhaps they didn't mind. The Scots were keen on both education and precision. "Precisely" was a word she heard often on the radio here. At least in the Palm Houses there were some explanations in English. The only Latin she could remember was *caveat emptor* and the opening of Caesar's *The Gallic War*. Her husband was able to read Latin — and Greek as well. She had been a student but he was a scholar; she found that out very early on.

"But you can't hold a tune," she would say to him later, after they were married. "The one fairy absent from your christening. When you sing you sound like a crow." "But you sing like an angel," he said. "You can sing for the two of us. Where we're going that's much more of an asset than being able to translate Virgil."

Music — singing — had been her passion. It was the reason she had gone regularly and willingly to church as a child and the reason she had continued to go long after she had lost her faith, long after she had come to regard the church as little more than theatre and her own particular church, the Presbyterian, as not particularly good theatre at that. She had sung in a choir from the time she was seven until she was twenty-eight and she still played the piano sometimes in the evenings, for her own pleasure, singing words she no longer believed in just for the delight in the music.

"Why did you run after me then?" he said, all those years ago, "if you thought I was an old crow in a kilt?" "Because you had wild, impassioned eyes." And that was the truth. When he spoke, when he was fired up about something, his eyes, which were dark blue, became the most dominant feature in his long, rather plain face. They held you. She could well imagine him as a fanatic or chieftain at Culloden or one of the student martyrs. He was full of conviction, which was more than she could say for herself. She had no idea where she was going, except back to America with her room-mate when this year in Scotland was over. Back to finish her degree and then marry some nice boy from Harvard or Amherst or Yale, have children, occupy herself with family and house and perhaps, if she were lucky enough to live near a good one, regular meetings of a choir. If she didn't marry she had no idea what she would do — graduate school, a career in publishing maybe, kind auntie to her older sister's children. She wanted something else, something more. She wanted a Destiny.

Within a week of seeing Gordon MacLeod, she was attending chapel regularly each morning and had joined the SCM. When she found out that he was going to be a missionary she joined the Afro-Asian Society as well. She danced with boys whose faces she later recognized in newspaper photos of independence celebrations. As yet, they had not exchanged a single word.

Now she stood for a moment outside the Palm Houses, elegant buildings of honey-coloured sandstone, virtually the only stone buildings in the city not dappled with grime. Perhaps they were sandblasted regularly or specially treated in some way. They had been built in the middle of the nineteenth century and the glass roofs, which went up in two rounded tiers in order to accommodate the height of some of the specimens inside, were strengthened with wrought iron painted white. They reminded her of the tops of fancy birdcages, or perhaps iron hairnets. She unbuttoned her coat and went in to the first house, the one that held the Temperate palms. The windows were steamed up and as she moved away from the entrance the smell rose up to meet her. It was really the smell she came for — rich, moist, sweet, excessive, the smell of West Africa. If she closed her eyes — if she closed her eyes and added the smell of charcoal burning. If she closed her eyes and added the smell of charcoal burning and the sound of someone pounding *fou-fou* near-by. She filled her whole being with the smell; it was like a drug. It was the smell that created the pictures.

Gordon stopped in the middle of a sentence and looked up. They were reading *Emma* out loud to one another by the light of the pressure lamp. The power had gone off again and the generator was being repaired.

"Where's that drumming coming from?"

He looked at her. "One of the boys borrowed Brother Aiden's old motorcycle and he had an accident."

"Brother Aiden?"

"The one who looks after the hens."

"Is the boy dead?"

"I'm afraid so. He was hit by a lorry. I imagine they are taking him back to his village."

"Will he have a Catholic burial?"

"Oh, I think so. But no doubt he'll have a traditional funeral as well."

She was very sorry, but in a distant way. He was not one of their boys and her pregnancy had advanced to the point where only those things which touched her life

directly held any great interest for her. Even her parents'
letters, when they arrived, would sometimes remain unopened for days before she got up the energy to read
them. Her world had contracted to the house they lived
in, with its sheet-metal roof and the louvred windows
tilted to catch any hint of a breeze, the mission school
where both she and Gordon taught from 7:30 A.M. until
noon and the market where she and a young girl named
Comfort, who boarded with them, went once a week to
get food. It was the dry season and the heat was terrific.
Her baby would be born before the first rains came.

At the mid-morning break the girls played jumping
games in the school yard. She couldn't imagine where
they got the energy.

> "Zacharias stole the meat from the cookin' pot."
> "Who me?"
> "Yes you."
> "Couldn't be."
> "Then who?"
> "Number Two. Number Two stole the meat from
> the cookin' pot."

They jumped and clapped their hands and shouted out
and then trooped back into the classrooms to learn about
the uses of the comma or the geography of Africa or why
it was important to take their Sunday-Sunday medicine.
The boys wore khaki shorts and white shirts; the girls
wore sleeveless checked gingham dresses which they
never seemed to zip all the way up the back. She
wondered if it were a fashion and told Gordon how, when
she was thirteen, most of the girls she knew wore their
cardigans buttoned up the back, she couldn't remember
why.

"Maybe it was to draw attention away from our
breasts, of which we were both proud and embarrassed.
Seems silly now, but it was all the rage one spring at West
Junior High."

"I love your breasts," he said then. "I love everything about your body."

It amazed her that he could say these things without embarrassment, surprised and moved her that he liked to put his face against her belly and wait for the baby to kick or shift position. The first time it moved she cried out. It felt as though she had swallowed a bird. Quickening. So that's what it meant. "As in 'from thence He shall come to judge the quick and the dead', " her husband said.

Sarah's parents had sent them money for a honeymoon and insisted it be used for such. Sarah thought they should save the money but Gordon disagreed. So they had gone to Ullapool for a week and stayed at a Bed and Breakfast rather than the youth hostel where they would have been in separate dormitories. But the couple who owned the B and B were terrible talkers — the husband had flown a Lancaster bomber in the war and liked to talk about it after dinner while the wife sat and tatted until exactly 10 P.M., when she said, "I think it's time for a milky drink," and disappeared into the kitchen. Each morning for breakfast she served them half a grapefruit with a palm tree stuck in the middle. The palm trees had celluloid trunks and crepe-paper branches. Sarah was convinced it was because they had said they were going out to Africa. Gordon thought it was some free offer she'd sent for from *Woman's Own* or one of the other ladies' magazines and it was done to impress. On the last morning, when Sarah asked if she could have one as a souvenir, the woman said no in a very huffy manner.

They were grateful that the landlady and her husband had their bedroom away at the bottom of the corridor. It was the end of the season and Sarah and Gordon were the only guests. He wasn't shy but Sarah was, very. She didn't like the idea of the other couple listening to them.

"Shh," she whispered, "or Mrs MacFarlane will come in and offer us another drink of Horlicks to help us sleep." The nightly hot-water bottle had been kicked out onto the floor. There was blood on the sheets, but not much, and Sarah quickly made the bed each morning directly after breakfast. Gordon didn't seem to mind any of this; what was it to him if these people talked about them or not? What indeed? But still Sarah wished they were in a nice big impersonal hotel. She insisted Gordon put the condoms in a paper bag which she threw away each day in the litter-bin on the front. Keep Scotland Tidy, it said on the bin. On the fourth night they lost a condom in the bed and searched frantically, ripping the bedclothes apart and ending up in hysterics after it was found. There was a knock on the door and the landlord's voice. "Is everything all right in there?" This made them laugh even harder, and after he'd been reassured and gone away, they had to put pillows over their faces until they calmed down. "Oh," she said, "won't it be wonderful, wonderful, wonderful, when we have a place of our own?"

The baby was born dead; somehow the cord had got twisted around its neck. It must have happened at the very last. Sarah couldn't seem to stop crying. One of the two nuns at the Catholic mission came to see her — Sister Patricia. She was a teaching sister, wore a shortish grey dress and drove a Jeep. She held Sarah's hand. "I don't know if this will really be of any help to you," she said, "but the people here believe that every baby has a ghost mother as well as a mother on this side. The ghost mother tries very hard to get her baby back, which is why new babies aren't given a name or even taken outside for nine days. If a baby dies, well, it has gone back to the ghost mother. I suppose it's trite to say that you are young and you will have other children, no doubt. I've never borne a child, so in a very real sense I can't possibly know what you are going through." She bathed Sarah's face and rubbed her temples with lemony smelling cologne and then she left.

Sarah was strangely comforted by the idea of the ghost mother, whom she saw as a young woman like herself, whose baby had been lost and now was restored. A smiling dark-skinned woman in a bright cloth. In dreams the ghost mother stood on the opposite bank of a narrow river. She held up the baby's hand to wave at Sarah. Sarah stopped crying.

The baby, named Morag after Gordon's mother, was buried in the small cemetery behind the church. The other teachers and all the students came to the ceremony. That night it was her husband who couldn't stop crying and she who became the comforter. As she held him her breasts leaked milk and it ran down onto his face. She held his mouth to her flowing breasts.

When she had made up her mind to marry him, her room-mate thought she was mad.

"You can't be serious."

"I love him."

"You are an incurable romantic. It was one thing to flirt with the idea of falling in love while we were over here but I can't see you as a missionary's wife. You don't go to church. You don't even believe. I can't picture you out in the bush somewhere reading Camus and Sartre while he converts the heathen."

"I believe in him. Isn't that enough?"

"Ask him. Ask him if that's enough. Has he proposed, by the way?"

"No, not yet. But he will."

In the second month she had found out he loved to dance. And so she began taking lessons in Scottish country dancing and attended the weekly ceilidhs with a Scots boy in their rooming-house. Gordon had a regular dancing partner, a pretty girl from the island of Lewis, who sang songs in Gaelic in a clear, tremulous voice. People who knew them assumed that they would marry. Sarah worked hard, practising the complicated patterns with the nice boy from the floor below. It was harder than square dancing because there were actual steps to learn and no one called out the moves. She had proper dancing shoes made of soft black leather. They laced up in an open-work way and tied around her ankles. The men wore them as well. She tried to imagine the boys she knew back home wearing shoes like that — they wouldn't be caught dead.

One night he was there without his dancing partner. The wind off the North Sea was bitter and many people were down with flu. The fiddle announced "Windin' Bobbins." Sarah had that one down cold. She saw Gordon looking around, took a deep breath, went up and touched his hand.

A week later she invited him to a Thanksgiving dinner some of the American students were organizing. She wore a black dress with a large white collar. "You look like a pilgrim," her room-mate said. She had invited the young doctor she was keen on. "I am."

What did he see when he said the word "God," the words "Our Father." They were walking hand in hand, their dancing shoes slung around his neck. He tried to explain. He kissed her.

Three days later she sent him some lines from a story by James Joyce. (They had been reading *Dubliners* together, sitting in the sunshine by the ruined castle.) The woman in Joyce's story had once held a bad opinion of Protestants, but had decided now that they were very nice people. A little quiet she thought, and serious, but still nice to live with.

And underneath these lines the single word, "yes."

In the Tropical Palm House a marmalade cat was asleep on the moist earth under a tree. It opened one eye in a lazy manner and sank back into sleep. She wondered if it had simply wandered in or belonged to one of the gardeners. This must be paradise for a cat used to the

chill of an Edinburgh winter. The rich smells in this house
were almost overpowering and here grew the real tropical
palms. One of them, a palm from New Guinea, was over
two hundred years old. Outside the glasshouses only
she — and the cat — would survive, but here the palms
flourished, and the passion flowers, all the lush tangle of
growing things that loved intense heat and humidity. She
always found the taller palms quite comical, like feather
dusters or strange one-legged birds. In the town where
she grew up there were no palms: chestnuts, oaks,
maples, larches, the trees of a northern climate. Once a
year in Sunday School, on Palm Sunday, the children
were given a few palm fronds to take home. The junior
choir sang, "There is a green hill far away," and outside,
after church, the boys swatted the backs of the girls' knees
with the palm fronds or swished them through the air like
imaginary swords. Sarah loved the look of them —
greeny yellow, exotic — and the feel, waxy and cool. She
always put her dime in the box for the church's work
abroad. The cross above the altar at the First
Presbyterian Church was bare, to show that Christ had
risen. When Sarah was confirmed, she received an Oxford Self-pronouncing Bible, Illustrated, with Questions
and Answers.

The second baby came months too soon. She and Comfort were sitting on the veranda, slicing green beans.
Comfort had begun reading *The Pilgrim's Progress* out loud
so that Sarah could help her with the more difficult words.
Comfort said, "the slow of Despond," and Sarah laughed, then hugged her so her feelings wouldn't be hurt.
"English," she said, "is a terrible language. I never
know quite how that should be pronounced, but I don't
think it's 'slow.' Slew or sluff. We'll ask Gordon when he
gets home." Then she offered to help with the mending,
to make up for laughing. Comfort was now fifteen and

could turn sulky. All of a sudden Sarah felt a strange rip-ping, or pulling away, inside her, and then the blood began pouring down her legs.

The baby was so small it would have fit in the palm of Gordon's hand. They gave it a name and buried it next to the other one. Vultures circled high up over the graves.

And now Sarah became afraid. When Gordon talked about Acts of God she told him she saw a golden axe, that this was the Axe of God, and that she was being punished. But she did not tell him why. Things that had not bothered her before began to bother her now — the sun, the snakes, the noise of drumming in a nearby village, the silly jumping games of the schoolgirls.

     "Zacharias stole the meat from the cookin' pot."
     "Who me?"
     "Yes you."
     "Couldn't be."
     "Then who?"

Certain words detached themselves from ordinary con-versation and floated on the wall above her head: "Knife," for example, or "fever" or "blood." Some-times she saw the Axe of God. One night, when it was her turn to read aloud, the letters in the words suddenly swarmed together, like a ball of soldier ants, and began to hum. She threw the book across the room and wept. Although he had his arms around her, her husband seemed to be very far away. "What is it, what is it, can you tell me what's the matter?" He asked for a year's leave and took her back to Scotland. On the ship she came out of their cabin only at meal-times and then she had to force herself to eat. "It won't make any difference," she told him, "whether we stay or go."

Orlando, the Marmalade Cat. He had gone to Paris, wearing a beret, and had thought they were selling poison in the fish shop. She still had all the Orlando books, tucked away at the bottom of the big chest in her front hall. She ought to get them out and give them to Eric across the stair. "If you are being punished," her husband said, "and I don't believe that for one minute, then surely *we* are being punished?" "No," she said, "*I* am being punished. It's nothing to do with you."

After they had been in Edinburgh for three months, and her blood count was back where it should be, she told Gordon she wanted to try for another baby. He was reluctant; he told her that it did not matter if they never had children, but she insisted. She knew he went to see a psychiatrist and that the psychiatrist told him to let her have her way. And once she was pregnant again everything dropped back into place. All that other — the fear, the strange detached words printed on the walls of their house, the inability to read — this was due to nothing more than depression and loss of blood. She began to go out again. They were living in the manse of the man who had taken Gordon's place for the year and every day Sarah walked from there to the Botanic Gardens to visit the Palm Houses. She was determined that they would return to Africa. All her love for her husband came flowing back, as though it had gone out with the haemorrhages and was now built up again, like her red blood cells. She slept with his head on her shoulder, his hand on her belly.

One day the postman brought a parcel and a note from Africa. The note was from the minister who was filling in. Everything was fine. The present was from Comfort. It was a wooden doll, about twelve inches high, with a cylindrical body and a large flat head. They knew what it was — an Akua'ba doll. In the old days young girls had been given these dolls at puberty and even wore them wrapped in a cloth on their backs, just like a real baby. They were fertility dolls. Sarah had written Comfort about the pregnancy and this was her gift. "This will be your Come and Stay Child," she wrote. "You wait and see.'' She added that everyone at school was praying for them both.

They put the doll on the mantelpiece, where it looked out of place with the other family's china dogs and family photographs. The doll was wearing a necklace of trading beads that Comfort must have bought in the market. It was quite beautiful, in a distant, hieratic way. ''Not at all like the dolls of my childhood,'' Sarah said, ''but then, it's not made for playing, is it? I wonder if it's Comfort's own doll?'' She was very touched and sent, with their next letter, a book of Celtic fairy tales and enough blue checked gingham for a new school dress. ''Dear Esther,'' she wrote, for Comfort now wished to be called Esther, ''Dear Esther, We are all fine here and looking forward to our return.''

The baby was born at the Royal Infirmary — an easy birth, a boy. Three months later, after Sarah was completely recovered and the child had been vaccinated, they took the train to Liverpool in order to sail back to Africa. In the customs shed, Sarah handed Gordon an envelope. ''I'm going to the Ladies,'' she said, ''read this while I'm gone.'' ''Shall I hold the baby?'' ''No,'' she said, ''he's coming with me. . . .'' Her husband didn't protest; no doubt he thought she couldn't bear to let the baby out of her sight.

''I have to do this,'' she said to the baby. ''You've got to understand, all right? It's either now or later on. I can't take any more. How do I know you're a Come and Stay Child? Look at you — pale and freckled — out there you'd last about five minutes.'' She hugged the baby tight as she walked up and down the far end of the quay. Gordon was inside, surrounded by old friends and colleagues, people who believed the way he did. He'd be all right, he had his faith.

The authorities decided, all things considered, not to press charges.

She was known in the Crescent as Mrs MacLeod, a widow, who might have been a missionary or a school teacher and who'd had some sort of a breakdown when she was very young. MacLeod was a common name. "Are you one of the MacLeods from Skye?" they would say and she would shake her head and smile. She kept to herself, had an income from some source, was pleasant and known to be good with children.

Late that night she lit candles in the elaborate brass holders on each side of the rosewood spinet she had inherited from her mother. Then she opened one of the tall windows which faced onto the Crescent, turned off the lights, and sat down to play. She started with Schubert, whom they both had loved. Schubert, Brahms, then the old hymns ("Once to every man and nation/Comes the moment to decide"). She had no doubt that he would try and find her. She was in the telephone book; it would be easy. But she had stopped her ears with cotton wool and closed the door to the lounge so that she could hear neither the doorbell nor telephone, nor any call that might come from the man she was sure was standing under the street-lamp below, listening to the music.

A Hunter's Moon

A Hunter's Moon

"Why do you keep on about it?" Annette said. "Why not just drop the subject?" Larry was all keyed up, leaning forward and gripping the steering wheel. When he glanced towards her his eyes actually glittered.

"But it came out of nowhere! We could have been killed! Did I run the light? I don't think I ran the light. Did I? Or did she?"

"I really don't know; I was napping. I suggest we listen to the radio or talk about something else."

"I have to talk about it — it helps me to get things out. When something like that happens I have to deal with it as soon as possible. It's like getting back up on a horse."

"Well, no, it isn't really like getting back up on a horse. You never got off the horse. And the horse wasn't out of control — as far as I can make out. As I said, I was taking a nap."

"Are you angry?" he said. She could see him smiling into the windshield. Larry was a man who smiled a lot and chuckled a lot, chuckle, chuckle, chuckle. Full of excitement and enthusiasm. If he weren't a Canadian he could have been Jack Armstrong the All-American Boy. And that would make her Betty, the All-American sidekick. Oh great.

"Aside from the fact that we nearly crashed into the side of that car and I was scared shitless, no, I'm not angry. I just wish we could get on to another subject or listen to some music." She reached over and fiddled with the dial until she got CKWX. A guy was singing that all his exes lived in Texas.

It wasn't true — about her not being angry. She was angry and a lot of other things besides. She should have left him at Horseshoe Bay and waited for the bus into town. Larry was stoned. He'd been stoned most of the weekend and had toked up just before they left Roberts Creek. She did not like to ride with people who were stoned, even when they insisted it sharpened their perceptions. She'd been stoned often enough in the old days to know that wasn't strictly true — one could be so easily distracted, by how the windshield wipers looked like long-legged birds in some curious mating dance, or how interesting and beautiful the ends of one's fingertips were. It also made you more casual about things, important things. (Oh wow, the baby's fallen into the water. Far out. Oh look, the cabin's on fire. Don't you love fire — it's so *elemental*. Hey man, we're going over the edge. This is *flying*!) She started her standard plea when in a dangerous situation: "Please God, I'll never be bad again if you'll just let me get out of this one."

While they were waiting for the ferry at Gibsons Landing Larry said, very excited, "You know, I couldn't sleep at all last night I was so turned on by Zöe. What an amazing woman! So real, you know, so natural." He smiled a little reminiscent smile. "I went for a walk in the moonlight, stark naked in all that long grass and the dew all over my legs. I even went and sat in the bath — it was still warm. I was *so* turned on!"

The car in the line-up in front of them had one of those

fancy B.C. licence plates you paid extra for. It said JAX.JILL. Their car window was open and the radio was playing golden oldies: "Love Letters in the Sand," "There's a Small Hotel," "These Foolish Things." Annette began to hum along with the music.

"I'm so high I don't know why I need this," he said sheepishly, rolling a joint.

"I don't either," Annette said. She was sitting right up against the window. "I hope we get on this sailing," she said. "It's the last one."

"We could always," said Larry, closing his eyes and drawing in the smoke, huh, huh, huh, then releasing it with a great sigh, "go back and stay another night."

"I have to get home, Nora's expecting me."

"She's seventeen, she'll be all right."

"I have to get home." But it was all right. They got on.

"How long have you known Zöe?" Larry said now, as they hurtled through the night to their doom.

"Would you mind slowing down," Annette said, "just a bit?" She had never found it much use to ask men to slow down when they were driving but it was worth a try. She really was frightened. (". . . in a seven-car pile-up on the Upper Levels Highway last night. Names of the dead have not yet been released.")

"I'm only doing the speed limit," he said, "same as everybody else. Well, just a little above — same as everybody else. That near-miss must have *really* shaken you up. Poor bunny. Just close your eyes and relax."

"That's what I was doing when you swerved, remember. Please slow down." The speedometer was broken on Larry's van; she had no idea how fast he was really going. "About five years," she said. "I've known her about five years."

She was much more angry and depressed at the possible end of her friendship with Zöe than she was at her disappointment in Larry. Larry was just Larry, someone who had been briefly — and deceptively — important.

The kind of person you'd be sorry, later, that you'd told the story of your life to, but there wouldn't be any real heartache involved. But Zöe — she would hate to lose Zöe. And it would be her decision, Annette's. Zöe probably wouldn't even know what she was talking about. There was no phone up there at Sven's, so confrontation would have to wait. Larry didn't mean a thing to Zöe, Annette was pretty sure of that. He wasn't even another scalp. Annette had known warrior-women and Zöe wasn't among them. She was simply used to men falling all over her. What Larry had done — and what she had done — would simply be normal behaviour to Zöe. ("But that was careless," Annette thought now, "she was careless of my feelings in a way I'm not going to be able to accept.")

"No phone!" Larry had said. "Amazing. I love to talk on the phone — for hours. Ask Annette." He smiled at Zöe. "I guess I'll just have to write you a letter."

Annette met Larry at a dinner party in Vancouver. He actually lived on Hornby Island but was in town for the winter, house-sitting for some actors he knew who had gone to Berlin. He made stained glass in his studio on Hornby but told her he had so many commissions he couldn't keep up with the demand. So he was more or less taking the winter off, except for one or two small things, and catching up on some reading, seeing films, renewing old acquaintances. He had a round, slightly breathless voice, very intimate, and when she left he came to the door with her and gave her a big hug and his phone number. Annette was what she and her best pal Zöe called "between friends," although really Zöe was never without a "friend" — at least one — for more than a few weeks, whereas Annette hadn't been with anybody for a couple of years. Annette was five years older than Zöe. Last year they had dressed up in Victorian clothes and marched in the annual peace march as "FUTURE

GRANNIES FOR PEACE'' and now they each had a grandchild. Zöe had been married at nineteen, Annette at twenty-two. They both got annoyed when people said, ''You don't look like grandmothers,'' and modified Gloria Steinem's classic reply, saying, ''This is what grandmothers look like these days.'' Zöe's last child was spending a year in England with his father; Annette's youngest daughter was in grade twelve. Young men often fell in love with Zöe and sometimes with Annette. Zöe was nicer to them than Annette was. They assumed, because she had raised three kids, that she was forever maternal and she did, in fact, feel quite kindly towards them, with their lovely bodies and intact dreams. But they were so unformed, somehow, and they praised her chocolate cake too much or said things, at the end of a meal, like, ''I'll do the dishes for you,'' which made Annette and her daughter Nora burst out laughing. Annette was a playwright — for both stage and radio; she often borrowed phrases and gestures from the young men for her plays. One thing that intrigued and appalled her was that most of them hated their mothers. When she mentioned this to Larry, who was not so young as he looked at first glance and had a sizeable bald spot on the top of his head, Larry said that he hated his mother as well.

''Why? Why all this hatred of mothers?'' Annette had an ecology sticker on the back bumper of her car. It was a picture of the earth plus the words, in large letters, LOVE YOUR MOTHER. One day her next-door neighbour, over eighty, said to her, pointing at the sticker, ''Why?''

''I beg your pardon?''

''Why should I love my mother? I hated the old bitch.''

''It means Mother Earth,'' Annette said. She pointed to the picture of the world.

''Oh,'' he said, and went back to raking up leaves.

''My mother nearly killed me,'' Larry said. It was a Sunday and they were walking along the sea-wall at Stanley Park.

"You mean child abuse? She beat you?"

"No, no. Nothing like that. There are more subtle ways. After my brother was born she ignored me completely. I think she actually neglected me, didn't feed me, stuff like that. I can remember wanting to die. I was awfully sick for a whole year."

"Do you really think she didn't feed you? How old were you when your brother was born?"

"Three."

Annette smiled at him. "Well then, I think it must have been an extreme case of jealousy. The first child has a hard time. I remember Sam crying and crying when it dawned on him that we were really going to keep Nora, that we weren't just minding her for somebody. But he got over it — eventually. Maybe it's harder if the second child is the same sex, I don't know. But it seems strange that you wanted to die. Anyway, it's time to forgive your mother, don't you think? Is she still alive?"

"Oh yes, but she doesn't approve of my lifestyle."

"Why don't you talk to her about all this. Or a shrink. Have you ever gone to a therapist?"

"I couldn't do that. I'm too quick. I'd know the reason behind the questions so I'd just feed him what he wanted to hear."

"Well, I'd talk to your mother about it."

"Do you really think I should?"

Larry had never been married, although he had lived with a woman once, for several years, in a communal situation up in the Kootenay Mountains. He told Annette how one of the women up there had a two-year-old kid. She and her man never shut the kid out when they wanted to make love. He played in a corner with his blocks, or if he felt like it he actually rode on the man's back. Nothing was hidden from that kid — everything was completely open and natural.

"Wonderful," Annette said. "Any idea where that kid is now? What he is like? Whether he loves his mother?"

"I lost touch with them after I left the commune. It was a really painful time for me so I just cut all the ties when I left."

"I see."

"My lady wanted some kind of commitment but I was too young for all that. You know how it was, back then." His "lady."

"No, not really. I was already very much married and committed when the Revolution started. Commitment was never one of my 'hang-ups.' As they used to say. Back then."

Annette asked herself why she was wasting her Sunday afternoon walking around the sea-wall with this asshole. Nora being away at her father's, Annette and Larry had slept together the night before. Then, in the morning, over coffee, he chuckled and said that was the first time he had ever slept with anyone and not been intimately involved in the process.

She put down her coffee cup and stared at him. "The *process*? Is that what it was? I had a good time, your penis seemed to be having a good time."

"That's just it! My penis was having a wonderful time. I hadn't had sex in over a month, I needed that, my body needed it. I feel great this morning. But I wasn't involved, somehow, not on a personal level."

"I see."

"Are you hurt?" he said. "I don't mean this to be hurtful. I didn't *not* enjoy it and my penis loved it." He smiled. He had nice teeth.

Annette got up from the table and went into her study and shut the door. You do not need this, she told herself. This guy is unreal. You are not that desperate: get rid of him quick. Then she did some deep breathing and went back to the kitchen.

"Hey, hey!" Larry said. He had toast crumbs at the corners of his mouth. "Are you okay? What were you doing in there?"

"Just putting something down in my notebook," she said and smiled sweetly. "Would you like me to make some more coffee?"

"Don't be spiteful," he said, "that's not like you."

"Oh I'm not being *spiteful*," she said, "I'm a professional. When I get handed a line like that it's too good not to put down in the little black notebook. And I find I forget things if I don't put them down right away. Say, I'll bet you envy your penis — having all that fun and you kind of left out of it, just there, like a UN observer. Perhaps I could make you a blue beret for such occasions."

"Do you take notes on all the stuff I tell you?"

"No dear, you're not that interesting." She could see that she now had the upper hand. "And don't get excited, I take notes on everybody. Let's get dressed and go for a walk."

He called her up two nights later. "Hi Annette, are you still awake? Listen, that stuff I told you about the coke, the marijuana plants, all that stuff."

"What about it?"

"Well, I'm in business, you know. I have a really successful business going."

"So?"

"So — well. I wouldn't want all that to be public knowledge."

"I see."

"Good. I'm glad you do, I was sure you would." Laugh laugh, chuckle chuckle. "It was silly of me to worry."

"Larry," Annette said, rolling over so she could continue watching "The Journal" and talk to him at the same time, "I don't believe I'm the only one you've told your life story to. I'm pretty sure, given your propensity for intimate conversation, that there are quite a few people who know about your marijuana plants and the coke and your mother's neglect of you and the beautiful young native girl you spent the night with, in the same bed, but didn't fuck because it was so intimate, so beautiful, so *magical*. I'm pretty sure, from the way you tell these things that they have been told before, several times before. Maybe it's a kind of courtship ritual, equivalent to the wild displays and hoarse cries of certain birds. I would have no qualms, therefore, about using anything you've told me; but believe me, it wouldn't be the tired old stuff about cocaine and marijuana plants. But I am discreet — if I ever used anything you've told me, no one would recognize you. Except you. Maybe. Someone might recognize your penis, however, I can't be sure of that. I can't guarantee anonymity for the penis and that little vein that appears to make your initial. You pointed that out to me, remember? But I can change the initial, that's easy — if I ever used that — so as not to embarrass your penis. So some woman, seeing a play, or hearing about a similar penis in the play, wouldn't say to herself — or her girlfriend — 'Hey! I know who this play is all about.' "

"You bitch. You really would pay me back for the other night, wouldn't you?"

"What other night?" Annette said. "Listen, I have to go now. Barbara and Bill are saying good-night to each other, I love this bit." She put down the phone.

Annette looked over at Larry. Could he possibly have speeded up? Can she make a citizen's arrest? Is there a special formula, certain phrases one is obliged to say? If she opens her mouth now and says, "I, Annette Weaver, do hereby arrest you for driving without due care and attention while under the influence of a mood-altering substance," what then? Would he really pull over, stop the car and meekly hand her the keys? And even if he did, ha ha, he'd have to pull over by a phone booth so that she could call the cops. But what if, which is more likely, he speeded up — or turned nasty? Years ago Annette said something accusatory to her about-to-be-ex-husband and he hauled off and smashed her in the eye.

That weekend, while the kids were staying with him, she went to a party with a publisher she knew. Annette had a terrible black eye but the publisher's girlfriend, a painter, thought it was wonderful. She got out her make-up kit and told Annette she'd turn the black eye into something outrageous, something everybody would want to have. Annette went along with it because she was afraid to be alone in the house, afraid of what she might do to herself if she stayed behind. The girlfriend had been right: everybody thought Annette's black eye was far out. But when the kids came back on Sunday night they were frightened; they couldn't believe their father would act in such a way.

There had been a one-sailing wait at the ferry going over so it was dark by the time they got to Zöe's and the moon was rising.

"We turn at this gravel road," Annette said, "and go to the end. Then we park the car and walk through the woods — not far."

"You've been here before?"

"I used to come here a lot, a few years ago. It's very beautiful."

Annette had written Zöe a letter and then Zöe had called from the general store. "I have no idea why I keep on see-ing him," Annette said, laughing. "But he came to Thanksgiving and was very witty and charming and had all the correct political views. And then on the weekend we ended up in bed together again and it was okay — nice. The earth didn't move but I did. And the stained glass he does is good — delicate, strong sense of colour, the real thing. I even ordered a piece for that old door I got at the wreckers. But maybe I'm just lonely. He analyzes everything, accent on the *anal*. Has weird dreams about his mother sticking her finger up his ass."

"Why don't you come up for a few days? There's a full moon on the seventeenth. We can sit out under the moon and talk this through. Anyway, I miss you."

"I miss you too. I'll see. It would be nice."

She told Larry she was going up to the Sunshine Coast for the weekend of the seventeenth. He offered to go with her. He could deliver some cupboard doors to a woman at Half-Moon Bay; she'd been waiting nearly a year.

"I'm not going that far — just a little beyond Gibsons. And I haven't seen Zöe in a while; I think it would be better if I went alone."

"I'll tell you what," Larry said. "I know you don't much like to drive so I'll go up with you and stay the night at Zöe's, if she's got room, and then go on to Half-Moon Bay the next morning. I'll come back Sunday and pick you up."

Why not? Maybe, if Zöe met him, she could give Annette some advice. She sent off a note c/o General Delivery, said she was coming and bringing "the friend." "I'll also bring some wine and all the gossip and some of those lovely dates from Galloways. Maybe we can do an exorcism. I'm not in love. Is this the way men feel? It hasn't happened to me before and I don't like it. He has an enormous capacity for hurting me; why is that if I'm not in love with him?"

Once they came out from the path through the forest, the moonlight was so bright it was easy to see their way past the big garden and along to the house. There were candles shining in the front windows and Zöe, laughing at the door.

"And about time too. I got so hungry I ate, but there's plenty for you two. Isn't it a perfect night? I started the fire under the bath at six — it should be just right by now."

Annette made the introductions, then Zöe told them to

sit down and eat. There was an open bottle of Sven's blackberry wine and Annette had brought two bottles which she placed on the table.

"What's this about a bath?" Larry said. "Do you mean a sauna? We have a lovely sauna on Hornby; I like saunas."

"It's a Japanese-style bath," Annette said, "outside by the garden. A big old claw-foot bathtub, really, with a pit dug underneath for the alder branches. There's decking to one side, and pitchers made by Sven. You wash yourself first, rinse yourself all over with the pitchers and only then, clean and shining, are you permitted to enter the bath, which has been filled hours before."

"The bath is a perfect size for two," Zöe said, "very romantic. You guys can steep out there in the moonlight and I'll sit nearby sipping wine and chatting." Zöe beamed at them, the good fairy. The kerosene lamp on the table enclosed them all in a puddle of yellow light. Since coming to the country Zöe had cut her black hair very short — it suited her.

"You should go pretty soon though. At midnight we'll eat blackberry pie."

Larry suddenly turned shy. "Oh, I don't know if I'm into an outdoor bath tonight. What if I just stay here and chat with you? I'm all keyed up." Keyed up was the right phrase, Annette thought, as he flashed his teeth at Zöe, like a pianist executing a fancy arpeggio. "You go ahead," he said to Annette.

Zöe stood up and grabbed Annette's hand. "Come on, you and I will go then. I'd love a bath with you in the moonlight." She poured them each another glass of wine. "Make yourself at home," she said to Larry. "There's a transistor radio, if you want to listen to something, and the outhouse is to the left of the path to the creek."

The two women went out, taking cotton kimonos off a hook by the front door. "Sven sent me some wild sage from the desert," Zöe said. "I put it in almond oil. It's fantastic in the bath."

The night was chilly now and the moonlight on the garden looked like hoar-frost. Zöe poured some of the sage oil into the bath, then they soaped each other, rinsed each other off and got in. Sven had made two wooden seats, like half-moons, so bathers wouldn't burn their ass on the bottom of the tub. The water was so hot Annette thought for a minute she might faint. It was a huge tub — a six-foot man could almost lie flat out. There was thyme and lavender around the decking and the water thrown from the pitchers had brought out the scent.

"Look," Annette said, "our bodies are steaming." She laughed. "Sure brings back memories." Annette had been one of Sven's girlfriends a few years back. It hadn't worked out but she still missed him, sometimes, and missed his place here in the woods. The year they were together Annette and Sven kept trying to think up a suitable name for the place. INN HOSPITABLE? INN COGNITO? After they began to quarrel one of their friends suggested INN COMPATIBLE.

Annette and Zöe faced each other in the bath, legs stretched out. The moon was yellow and huge. "Oh bliss," Annette said, "bliss bliss bliss." She sank down until the water was up to her chin and rubbed her big toe up and down the inside of Zöe's leg.

"Larry seems okay," Zöe said. "A bit *noisy* maybe. Perhaps that's what the city does to him."

"I think that's what the dope does to him. You know, when I met him I thought he was gay. But he's not — at least not in any way he's conscious of. And what do I mean by such a stupid statement?"

"Is he a good lover?" Annette told her about the penis remark. "What do you make of that?" The heat of the bath plus the wine had made Annette feel boneless, completely soft and silky. She could easily have fallen asleep. She didn't really want to talk about Larry just then.

Zöe laughed. "I used to know a guy on Gabriola Island like that. Very attractive but going through some weird times. He was married to a tiny little woman named

Dawn or Sunshine or Star — I forget. Something like that. Sunflower, I think it was. They were saving their money so he could go down to California and do primal screaming. You remember how it was — we all wanted to get back to our lost innocence. Well, he found me wandering in the woods on the anniversary of George's death, which turned out to be this guy's thirtieth birthday as well, so what with one *tristesse* and another we lay down on the leaves like the Babes in the Woods and fucked. *I* thought it was very pleasant, just what the doctor ordered, but as he was pulling up his pants, he said, "You have to realize that didn't mean anything." She finished off her wine. "We should have brought out another bottle. Come to think of it, he also was a man who hated his mother. That's why he was so anxious to get down there to California and scream."

"Did he ever make it?"

"I have no idea."

"Why do they all hate their mothers?"

"I don't know. Because mothers are so powerful I guess."

"But that means they hate women like us."

"Listen Annette, do we really like *them*? I'm not talking about sex, I'm talking about *like*."

They could see Larry coming along the path from the house, carrying his glass and a bottle of wine. "Aha," Annette called, "Ganymede — and just when we need you. We must have summoned you up. More wine, more wine, more wine!" They held their glasses up.

"I wouldn't sit there," Zöe said, "unless you want wet pants. That's where we perform our ablutions."

So he stood over them, looking down. "You ladies seem to be having a good time. Catching up on a lot of gossip?" He was both arrogant and obviously nervous, no doubt wondering what they had said about him.

"No ladies here," Zöe said, "just women."

"What a fantastic moon!" he said. Any minute now he would break into song.

"The Hunter's Moon," Zöe said. "It's got other names but I can't remember them."

"Maybe I should strip off and join the two of you."

"Not enough room," Zöe said. "It ceases to be comfortable. But I should go back now — there's a magazine article I want to finish reading before I go to bed. And I'll go get the ice-cream for the pie."

"Ice-cream? You don't have a fridge, do you?"

"No no, no electricity at all. But clever Sven has made a concrete box right at the edge of the creek. The water laps against it and keeps things cold. I saw a bear down there the other night. I think he was as surprised to see me as I was to see him. I just stood still on one side of the creek and he stood still on the other. Then he lumbered away up the water line."

"A bear!" Larry said, very excited. "What kind of a bear? You could have been killed!" (At least he didn't say, "Gosh," Annette thought.)

"Oh, I don't think so. I did put a chair against the door handle and told the neighbours the next day. They said they'd never seen or heard of a bear down here before. And Sven never said anything about bears."

Larry was staring at Zöe's body. She had beautiful breasts, with dark nipples. "Is Sven your lover?" he asked. Zöe laughed. She stood up in the bath and her entire body was outlined in an aura of steam.

"Occasionally." She reached for the towels she had wrapped around hot bricks. "Here. Your turn now."

"Oh, I think I'll just go back with you," Larry said. "On the off-chance I might see that bear."

Annette laughed.

"Let's all go in, then," Zöe said. She handed Annette a towel. They dried themselves off and put on kimonos. Larry went away into the garden, exclaiming over the pumpkins and squashes and anything else he could think to exclaim over. The women ran barefoot over the wet grass. "I hope he kept the stove going," Zöe said. ("If there were a ferry at this time of night," Annette thought, "I would take it.")

They sat on the big double bed, in their kimonos, a soft woven blanket over their knees. Larry lay on the bed, propped on one elbow, watching them, watching Zöe. Every so often he would shake his head and say, "Incredible!"

"I was looking at last year's diary," Zöe said to Annette, "after Gordon was up here last weekend. Then I wrote in this year's after he left, 'Annette was right.' "

Now Larry turned on his elbow and looked at Annette. Then he turned back to Zöe. "Right about what?"

"Oh, this lover of mine, a man Annette's known for years and years; he was her lover at one point. She said something perceptive about him, before he and I got together, and I wrote it down. Last weekend I realized just *how* perceptive she had been."

"What did she say?" Zöe shook her head and smiled. Annette had no idea what she had said about Gordon. Larry began rubbing his hand up and down Zöe's leg, under the blanket. Annette waited for her to tell him to stop. "Amazing! Have you two shared a lot of the same men?"

"Sure thing," Annette said, "we pass them back and forth all the time. The ones worth sharing that is." ("Why are you talking like this?" she said to herself. "Can't you hear what you sound like? And it's not true. It's true about Sven but it wasn't exactly 'sharing.' And I only slept with Gordon twice. What did I say? I'll ask Zöe tomorrow when he's gone.")

"Do you believe in committal?" Larry said to Zöe. "Umm," he said. "Your skin is so soft."

"I believe it's time for bed," Zöe said. "It's bed I believe in. Especially if you want to drive up to Half-

Moon Bay and back tomorrow.'' She turned to Annette.
''I thought you two could have the loft — it's more
private. I've put candles up there and a hot-water bottle
in the bed.''

''Oh Zöe,'' Larry said, ''that's so sweet of you. But
Annette and I generate so much body warmth when we
sleep together all night that I think we'd be better sleeping
apart. My sleeping bag's in the van so I think I'll go get it
and just curl up here on the rug.''

(''Here we go again,'' Annette thought. ''She can't
help it, I know, but it hurts.'') She went to the sink,
poured water from the bucket into a mug, took her
toothbrush and went outside. She could hear Larry's
stoned laugh and Zöe's low reply. Men always fell in love
with Zöe — why had she thought this would be any different? They met her at a party or a conference or on a
protest march and the next day they arrived at her door
with poems or flowers or beautiful hand-thrown pots.
Yet, in the end, Zöe herself always chose men who were
unsuitable in some way or other. Until six months ago she
had been with a younger man whom she adored and
whom the rest of her friends thought pushy and im-
mature, a hustler. At last year's communal Thanksgiving
dinner Zöe's boyfriend said ''real work'' occurred where
you got out there and worked with your hands, got bruised
and dirty. Annette asked if Marx had actually got out
there with the peasants, or Lenin?

''Listen,'' he said, ''real work happens when you go
out of the house in heavy boots and old pants and come
home exhausted.'' Annette was holding a pile of plates
and she was tempted to bring it down on his head. Zöe
was extremely political and yet she just sat there and
smiled. Annette figured Zöe must tune out when he made
stupid remarks like that. Two weeks later he told Zöe over
the telephone that they had to break up because he needed
to meet a younger woman and have children. Zöe had
been ready to marry him and still cried when she talked

about it. Which was why she was so happy to be out of the city for a while, working on her thesis and minding Sven's place while he went off to the desert.

Larry was falling for Zöe and he didn't care if Annette knew it. Why should it matter? Larry was weird. But if they started making love in there she was going to sleep in the van.

Annette threw away her toothbrush water, then went inside and through the door up to the loft, calling, "Good-night," over her shoulder.

"Hey," Zöe called, "don't I get a good-night kiss?"

"Kiss-kiss," Annette said, "smoochie-smoochie. See you all tomorrow."

Half an hour later she heard Larry slide open the door and come up the steps. She pretended to be asleep. He got into bed with her, naked, and began whispering in her ear. "I know you're not asleep, Annette, I know you're not. You hurt Zöe's feelings by your abrupt departure. She's still awake down there, reading. Do you want to come down?" He slid his fingers into her and laughed. "Oh ho, what have we here? All nice and juicy. Come on, Annette, I know you're not asleep!"

She kept her back to him while he lit the candle, then lay back down and began fucking her from behind. She willed herself not to say a word, to think about something else, the nine times table, which she'd always had trouble with, dialogue for her new play, the names of all the states in the United States, the conjugation, in French, of all the forms of the verb "to be." Finally she told herself it was Sven fucking her. He too would have smelled of wine and dope. They had often come up here in the afternoons, to lie together, so if anyone dropped by it would look as though they weren't home. She missed Sven. He was a wonderful lover and until they started quarrelling she thought at long last this was it.

"There!" Larry said, when she came. "Don't tell me

you're asleep.'' After a few minutes, when she said
nothing, he blew out the candle and went back
downstairs. Was this some kind of power trip? Would he
display his dripping penis or what? She heard him say
something but didn't hear a reply. Zöe might be indifferent to him but would she let him sleep with her just the
same? Would he dare to go down there and say, ''She
sent me back to you.''

Annette had told Sven, ''I'm sorry, I can't share.''
That's when the fights began.

''Why a 'green-eyed' monster?'' she thought, as she
fell asleep. ''Why green with jealousy? I feel purple with
it, bruised, swollen.''

In the morning, as they ate pancakes together, Larry
draped his left arm across Zöe's shoulder, his fingers just
above her breast. He suggested all three of them do the
drive to Half-Moon Bay.

''I've brought some work,'' Annette said, ''you two go
and I'll keep the home fires burning.''

''I've got to work as well.''

The neighbours' children appeared at the door — their
mother wanted to borrow some buckets for the last black-
berries. ''Is that your husband?'' the little girl asked Zöe.

''Of course not,'' Zöe said. ''I haven't got a
husband.'' Larry looked terribly pleased. After he finally
left, Zöe shook her head and laughed. ''That guy!''

''Did you sleep with him?'' Annette said. Her hands
were shaking so she couldn't pick up her coffee cup.

''Of course not. What do you take me for?''

''I'm not sure what I take you for. I'm going for a
walk.''

''Do you want me to come with you?''

''Go do your work.'' She put on her shoes and spent
the day sitting on a log at Roberts Creek. What she really
wanted was some peace and quiet in herself. But how to
accomplish it? She was not casual enough, had never

been casual enough. She felt like putting a message in a bottle and throwing it out to sea. "Help me." Help me do what?

Suddenly Larry slowed down and pulled off the road at a viewpoint. The moon looked as full and yellow as it had the night before. They got out and leaned on the rail, not touching, looking up at the moon. "Look," Larry said. Another car was there. It was the car with the corny licence plate and the couple who owned it, maybe sixty-five, had turned the radio up and were out there waltzing, underneath the Hunter's moon. "Hey, hey," Larry called to them, as he and Annette got back into the van. "Way to go, I love it!"

Ascension

Ascension

Christine hadn't prayed in fifteen years, but now she prayed in a steady monotone of pleading as she kneaded and turned the bread. Please don't let her die please don't let it happen — knead, knead, then a quarter turn just as Mrs Papoutsia had taught her — please don't let her die. She tried to imagine God as Mrs P must see him, a bearded patriarch in black robes and black beard with a hat like a piece of stove-pipe. Okay, please, for my sake. She hastily, guiltily, corrected herself — I mean for her sake. Knead, turn; knead, turn: for all our sakes, Amen.

When the siren went, Christine was lying on the bed, half-asleep. She thought it was the end of the world, shoved her feet into her slippers, ran downstairs and outside on to the wet grass. One of the volunteers from the south end of the island was just closing the doors of the ambulance. Christine ran across her yard and into the road shouting, "Stop, stop, what's happened?" He waved at her and slapped at his chest, then hurried around the passenger side. The vehicle sped away down the access road and on to the main road south. Wa Wa Wa Wa Wa Wa Wa. She could hear the dreadful sound as the ambulance raced towards the water-taxi.

It couldn't be too serious, Christine thought, or they would have got the helicopter or the Hovercraft. The government wharf was just down below and from time to time, even in the few months she had been on the island, a resident or weekender was taken off white-faced and, even if conscious, *vacant* somehow, as though the easiest way to deal with pain and fear and being in a horizontal and helpless position in full public view (not much public really, only those who lived close by and had heard the helicopter or Hovercraft coming in) was to absent oneself from the body which was causing all the trouble. Christine had seen the weekender who had chopped his finger off taken away like that, the finger in a plastic bag full of ice beside him. The injured man had seemed braver than the people around him, but of course he was in shock. He was a popular man and he put an ad in the local newspaper later on, thanking people for calls and cards and flowers: "Finger and hand reunited and doing fine." She had seen them take away Mr Jenks, the plumber, who had been up on his roof replacing shingles when his foot slipped and he fell off the roof and broke his back.

The faces of the sick or injured were as grey as wasp nests, grey as ashes. And the awful noise. Surely the noise would make one sicker, more frightened? Wa Wa Wa Wa Wa. She could still hear it. The ambulance must be at Smugglers' Cove by now. All along the route people would stop what they were doing, turn to one another or pick up the telephone. Who was it that just went by? "Hello, Muriel, did you hear the ambulance just now?" Christine remembered a poem she had read in second-year university: "The Hound of Heaven." A powerful religious poem by a man half-crazy from despair and opium. But, said her teacher, a man who never lost his faith.

> I fled Him, down the nights and down the days;
> I fled Him, down the arches of the years; . . .

A shocking poem because she had been brought up, like everybody else she knew, to think of Heaven and Christ in gentler terms. Excess in anything, but especially religious fervour, was frowned upon. "Gentle Jesus meek and mild" was the Christ she knew.

The ambulance sounded like Thompson's Hound of Heaven. But perhaps it wasn't so bad that it made that noise after all — all human terror gathered into the single scream of the ambulance siren. Faint now, but she could still hear it. And Mrs Papoutsia inside.

"Christina," Mrs Papoutsia said. "Nice name. Means golden one. Friends in Greece — lady friends — say, *'chrysomou'* — my golden one."

"It's Christine, not Christina."

"Same thing."

Christine stood in the wet, winter-logged grass, uncertain what to do. She wanted to go down to the store and find out more but was afraid to seem nosy. "Bread," she thought now, "it's Thursday. She must already have started the bread." Still in her wet slippers she went into Mrs Papoutsia's yard and up the back steps, searched for the key which she knew was hanging on a cup hook under the bathroom window and let herself in. The big black woodstove was still throwing off heat and two large earthenware bowls, covered with clean tea-towels, sat on the warming shelf. The room had the slightly sour smell of yeast and rising bread plus the liquorice smell of oil of anise.

Mrs P's two cats glared at her from the tops of cupboards. They were still shaken by the invasion of strangers and the awful sound.

"It's okay guys," she said, "you can come down." The cats continued to glare.

(''What are their names?''

''Perché.''

''Both of them?''

''Sure. Perché in Greek mean 'why' and also 'because.' One cat 'why' and the other 'because'.'' The old lady grinned, showing her gold-capped teeth. ''Is joke.'')

Christine lifted the heavy bowls down from the top of the stove and set them on the counter. She pulled off the towels and the waxpaper underneath. The dough had risen right up to the top and almost over the edge. She was just in time. She punched the dough down, hard, and it let out a little whoosh of air and a slick-slick sound when the bubbles burst. Christine knew enough about Greek bread by now to know, from the anise, that this was probably Easter bread. Next week Mrs P was going to show her how to make it. But what came after it rose again? Naturally there were no recipe books lying around. It would be a fancy bread, today of all days. It had to be braided and have hard-boiled eggs baked in the centre of it, or were those put in after the bread had baked? Christine looked in the fridge; there was a bowl of six bright red eggs already boiled and dyed. One problem solved at any rate. But did they go in before, or after?

Mrs P could not believe her new neighbour didn't know how to make bread.

''You never?''

''Never ever. I like good bread, but I guess I've always lived where I could get it from a bakery.''

''Your mama, no?''

''No. Never. She made good baking-powder biscuits and wonderful pancakes, but we bought our bread. I even remember the name of the bakery because it sponsored a music show on the radio.'' Christine began to sing, to the ''Tales from the Vienna Woods'':

> The famous Spalding Bakery
> A name that stands for quality
> We invite you to buy
> We invite you to try
> Delicious and pure Spalding Bread.

She laughed. "The songs they played were golden oldies — Frank Sinatra, Perry Como, stuff like that. My grandmother must've baked bread though. I remember long cylindrical hinged pans in the back of the kitchen cupboard." Her mother had given the pans to a church sale.

"Your grandmama good woman."

"My mother good woman too. She just didn't bake bread." Sometimes, when she talked with Mrs P she found herself leaving out parts of speech and wondered if the old woman thought she was mocking her.

"Staff of life — bread."

"Is that a Greek saying too? I mean, I've heard it all my life but do people in Greece say it as well?"

"In Bible! Isaiah! You no go to church?"

"I used to. I don't go any more."

"You don't believe?"

"Not any more."

Mrs P snorted. "Belief also staff of life."

"Maybe." The old woman gave her a hard look.

"You have nice voice. Why not join choir here? Not church choir, other one. Thursday night at Activity Centre. Meet people. Lovely to sing."

"I'm not staying long enough," Christine said. "There's no point."

When Christine came to the island in the New Year she had already made up her mind not be overly friendly with her neighbours, whomever they turned out to be. After all, she was only renting for six months. She'd be gone by

Canada Day. Besides, she was there to puzzle out certain things and the fewer complications the better. She had seen the ad in the *Times-Colonist* and answered it on a whim. She made all the arrangements before she told her friends. She also told them not to come and visit. Yeah, sure, they said. You'll get cabin fever in three weeks. You'll be on the phone begging us to come over or you'll be back here every weekend. But they were wrong. It was now the middle of April. She plugged the phone in only once a week, on Sunday mornings, to call her mother in southern Ontario. She did not answer letters, although she might have answered the one letter that never came.

"Where husband?" Mrs Papoutsia said. "Where childrens?"

"No children," Christine replied. "No husband. Not any more. Husband gone." Mrs Papoutsia dipped her cookie in her tea.

"You like nice Greek husband? My son arrange. He knows all Greek mens in Vancouver. He knows Greek mens in Greece."

"No thanks, I'm happy right now the way I am."

"What you do to husband that he leave?"

"What did *I* do! I didn't do anything."

"Hmnph."

Mrs P had a calendar from Greece above the kitchen sink. White stone houses that looked as though they had been dipped in the same powdered sugar she used for her raisin cake, her *kourabiethes*, her sesame turnovers. There were bright geraniums in pots and impossibly blue skies. "April" showed an old-fashioned windmill and two smiling men with a donkey. The simple life. But Christine knew that calendars could lie. She had lived in a city famous for its hanging baskets and old-world charm. Pictures of the teen-age prostitutes never graced the dozens of calendars produced each year.

Michael had been gone for nearly a year and still she couldn't fall asleep right away, no matter how tired she was and still she dreamt of him, strange, disturbing erotic dreams. The first day she got here, after she had unpacked her things, she took her wedding ring out of its velvet-lined box, walked to the end of the government wharf and threw it in. She hoped no fish would swallow it, no fisher-man appear at the door one day, wondering if she'd lost something. Their initials were on the inside.

"Listen," Michael said, "there's no nice way of saying this. I'm sorry." At least there were no children, her friends said, it's far worse if there's kids involved.

Christine gave the dough another big *thump*, turned it over to keep it oiled, replaced the paper and towels and put the bowls back on the shelf. Then she went down the steps and under the house for more wood. She felt she had to finish the bread, keep the fire going, if Mrs Papoutsia was going to have any chance at all, that Mrs P would count on her doing this. The bread was for Greek Easter, only two weeks away. Mrs P was having a big feast for everybody at the North End Hall. Her son was coming over to roast the lamb. When Mrs Papoutsia told her this it sounded like "Roast Lamp."

Had anyone called her son? Emergency numbers plus the son's telephone number and a few other numbers were posted neatly by the telephone. Everything in the small house was neat and tidy. On the window-sill by the back door there were clam shells, oyster shells, even walnut shells full of flower seeds to be planted as soon as the ground dried out a bit more. The little slips of paper identifying them were written in Greek but Christine could recognize a few of them by their shape: marigolds, cornflowers, nasturtiums. Glass jars held bean seeds and tomato seedlings were already sprouting on the front window-sill.

Paper bags were neatly folded in a corner of the cup-board underneath the sink, rubber-bands and twist-ties saved in the kitchen drawer. Everything that could be used again was used again; very little was thrown out.

Christine thought of her own untidy life. If something happened to her, her friends and her mother would have a terrible time sorting things out. "I must get a divorce as soon as possible," she thought now, opening the fridge and taking out the cat food. The two cats, both huge grey blue-eyed Persians, were Mrs Papoutsia's big indulgence. That and making breads and cakes. "I must give my life some order." She had taken a leave from teaching, on the grounds of illness. She had been experiencing dizzy spells at work and strange headaches. It was like being hit in the head with a snowball, she told the doctor, a sudden pain and then a dull ache. It scared her. The doctor sent her for tests but they all came back negative. She wept and he offered her a choice of Librium or Valium, "just until you pull yourself together." She declined and answered an ad.

There was quite a crowd at the store, discussing Mrs Papoutsia. She'd had a bad pain in her chest and called the doctor. It was lucky she did, because by the time he arrived with the ambulance she was lying on her bed in great distress.

"Did she call you?" the storekeeper said, noticing Christine.

"My phone was unplugged," she said and felt her face go red. Had she called? Christine imagined the doctor and the paramedics trying to get Mrs Papoutsia's heart to go, thumping it hard the way she had thumped the bread. Thump. Thump. "Where did they take her?" Christine asked. In spite of her shame and embarrassment she had to know. She bought some milk she didn't need and a Kit-Kat bar to give her visit some validity.

"Probably to the Royal Jubilee — if it's a heart attack. The doctor will know."

Christine went back up her path, called the doctor and got his wife. He was with Mrs Papoutsia and they were on

their way to Victoria, perhaps even there by now. "She
has a son in Vancouver," Christine said, "do you know if
he's been called? He runs a delicatessen on Broadway."

"I don't know. Shall I have Jim call you? He'll phone
in for messages pretty soon."

Christine left the son's number, which she'd copied
down, and also her own. It wasn't time to punch the
dough again and then attempt to braid it. She didn't even
know what temperature to use. The dough had eggs in
it — did that mean a higher or lower temperature?
Christine had so far attempted nothing more difficult
than round white loaves and something Mrs Papoutsia
called *"starénio,"* or "peasant bread," which was dark
and dense and wonderful spread with Greek honey
brought over by the son, who wore the nails of his little
fingers very long — to show that he did not work with his
hands. He called himself Mr Pappas. Mrs P loved him
fiercely but was impatient.

"Father fisherman, grandfather fisherman, good job,
honourable. Now he wants make sure everybody know he
don't work rough work. And change name! Easier for
peoples, Mama. No trouble. Papoutsia *easy* name!
Pa — poots — see — a." She grinned at Christine.
"Husband Dmitri, English 'Jimmy.' His name in
English Jimmy Shoes. I, Fotula, Mrs Jimmy Shoes."

Fotula and Dmitri had come to the island every year
when the herring were running. Their son, with scuba
equipment, dove for octopus. Fotula and Dmitri decided
to buy a small lot and build. Now that Dmitri was dead,
the son and his wife wanted Fotula to come and live with
them but she refused. There were no grandchildren. On
the island Mrs P was "Yia yia," "Grandmother" to a
couple of dozen little ones. She fed them sweetcakes ooz-
ing honey and nuts, wiped their sticky faces, kissed them,
rocked them in her rocking chair. They saw her coming
and ran to her with their arms outstretched.

"His doorbell play four tunes including Greek anthem. So what? Jimmy good boy but modern. Electric this, electric that. I no like."

Christine had very pointedly kept herself to herself and after a few weeks the neighbours accepted that she really meant it when she said no to morning coffee or afternoon tea, no to darts, no to the garden club, the women's auxiliary to the firehall, no to Scottish country dancing. (Mrs Papoutsia did Scottish country dancing every Tuesday night.) When Christine talked to people she felt that any second now she would crack and fall to pieces right before their eyes. She said she was writing a book and couldn't be disturbed. She was then invited to join the writers' group but declined. It was a book for teaching English as a Second Language, she said, not a creative book at all.

On the third Thursday someone knocked hard on the front door. An old woman stood on the porch, black skirt, black cardigan, black stockings and boots. She smelled of fresh bread and, faintly, of oranges. "Fotula Papoutsia," she said. "Your neighbour. I tell landlord I keep eye. Also clean on Fridays."

"Thank you very much," said Christine, who had been brought up never to be rude to elderly people, "that won't be necessary. I'm fine." The old lady walked right in and put something wrapped in a towel on the kitchen table. Delicious smells came up from under the towel. "Look," said Christine, trying not to sound annoyed. "It's awfully kind of you but —" The red kettle was being filled, the tea cannister taken down from the lefthand cupboard.

"Mr Beldon and me — tea or *kaffes* together Thursdays, bread day. He keep eye on me, my eye on him. You have jam?" She opened the fridge and peered in. "Next time I bring."

Christine took a deep breath. "Mrs Papoutsia, I don't know what your arrangement was with Mr Beldon, but I'm here to be very quiet — no visitors."

"Crazy talk," said the old woman, pouring hot water into the teapot and swirling it around. "Me, I *prefer kaffes* — cof-fee — but Joe he like tea. Come, sit."

A warm loaf, butter, teapot, teacups and saucers. "Sit, eat." When Christine began to cry, Mrs Papoutsia ignored her for a long while, sipped her tea, and buttered slices of bread, looked around the untidy room and muttered foreign words to herself. Finally, "*Andaxi*. Okay. You and me, we talk."

Now Christine felt the old panic returning — Mrs P, her one friend, her support, had been taken away. She was learning to make bread, to understand the mysteries of yeast, of how the milk had to be scalded, the water just the right temperature. When she kneaded and turned, kneaded and turned, kneaded and turned, she felt the anger and hurt leaving her, even if, as yet, it only left for a while, one day a week.

"You can even," said Mrs P, "get yeast out from air. I show you."

On bread-lesson days it was usually dark by the time Christine walked back to her own house, her basket full of Greek food she had sampled during the afternoon. When Mrs Papoutsia told her about the Easter Feast at the North End Hall and had asked — demanded — Christine's help, she had felt strong enough to agree.

"Easy food. Greece not a *fancy* place. Cheese. Olive. *Dolmades*, little pies of spinach, son do the lamp outside. Easter bread — I show you."

Christine dialled the hospital in Victoria. Yes, they had a Mrs Papoutsia in Intensive Care. Her son had just arrived. No, they could tell her nothing if she wasn't kin.

Was she conscious?

"I'm afraid I can't —"

Christine was shouting into the phone. "Well if she *is* conscious could you tell her, could somebody get word to her that Christina — yes, *Christina*, I'm her next-door neighbour — has seen to the bread The *bread*. That's right. Tell her Christina has seen to the bread.''

The son called just as Christine was taking the loaves out of the oven. The braids weren't even but they didn't look half-bad and she had been right to set the coloured eggs in before baking. She carefully put the hot pans on the racks she had already set out. The cats had come down and were watching her with a kind of angry interest. Where was their mistress — what had Christine done with her?

''Hello,'' Christine said, her own heart bumping loudly against her chest.

''Christina? Jimmy Pappas here. I tried your house then figured you'd be at my mother's.''

''How is she?''

''She just slipped away. We lost her about fifteen minutes ago.''

''Did she get my message about the bread?''

''She never regained consciousness.'' She could hear him struggling to keep his voice manly, in charge. ''I'll come over tomorrow. Do you think you could feed the cats and keep an eye on things?''

''We'll have to have the Easter Feast,'' Christine said. ''She'd want us to have the Easter Feast.''

''Thank you for being such a good friend to her Christina — she often talked about you.''

Christine hung up the phone. While the bread cooled she rinsed the pans and bowls and tidied the kitchen. Then she walked around looking at all the framed photographs on the walls: Fotula as a young girl; Fotula in her wedding dress with the six petticoats underneath; Fotula and Dmitri on their fish boat, *The Ariadne*; Fotula with young Dmitri in her arms. In none of the pictures was she smiling but there was a kind of fierce smile implied in the eyes, the mouth, the way she carried herself. A proud woman. Fulfilled.

And then, the most amazing photograph of all —

Fotula shaking hands with an astronaut. She was all in black, as usual; he was wearing white. It was the only photograph in which she smiled. The astronaut was smiling too.

"Is that your son?" Christine asked when she first noticed it.

"No. No. Mr Somebody — I forget name but I have clipping somewhere. I win big prize, go to Ottawa, meet astronauts."

"You won a big prize? Was it a lottery?"

Mrs Papoutsia gave her a look of contempt. "What you mean *lottery?* I enter contest — think up good project to try out in space, project to benefit mankind."

"And?"

"And I win! Make bread in space," I say. "If go to new worlds need staff of life — try make bread in space." Mrs Papoutsia and four others with the same idea had won the contest and been given the royal treatment. That wasn't all — they were to go to Cape Canaveral when the experiment actually went up. Mrs P had been looking forward to it enormously. If it hadn't been for the Challenger she would have gone already.

Christine sat in the rocking chair with one cat on her lap, the other at her feet. She had banked the fire in the stove and shut down the damper. The house smelled wonderful and in spite of her grief and shock Christine couldn't help smiling as she imagined the soul of her friend, fragrant, spicy, lighter than air, gradually rising up through the April skies towards a bright blue heaven.

In the Groove

In the Groove

His father took another toke, held it, exhaled with a deep, contented sigh. "Ribet," he said, "ribet, ribet. Lonesome Creek sure doesn't live up to its name. Our friends out there don't sound lonesome and we're not lonesome, are we?" He extended the joint to Josh. "You want a bit of this?"

"No, thanks." He hadn't meant to sound so disgusted but Josh didn't like it when his dad smoked up. He got this real soft smoky voice and always wanted to talk about LIFE. Whenever he got a letter from Charlie, he could tell by the contents, if not the handwriting, whether or not his father was stoned when he wrote it.

"Are you warm enough?" Charlie asked. They were sitting outside the tent, by their small fire. Josh nodded his head. Charlie had brought along his mouth harp (it was no good bringing a guitar on the motorcycle) and for the last while he'd been playing all the Golden Oldies. When he played "Runaway," Josh joined him on the kazoo. Charlie told Josh that once, back in the sixties, he and a group of fifty friends had performed all of

Beethoven's Ninth on kazoos. He liked to talk about the sixties and Josh liked to listen. The evening had been great up to now, but Josh sensed a bout of LIFE-talk coming on.

"Brr," Charlie said. "You can tell it's August when the sun goes down. Sure you're warm enough?"

"I'm sure."

Josh threw a stone into the fire. He knew it was a dangerous thing to do; the stone could explode. "Somethin' troublin' you, Josh?" That's another thing his father did when they went on trips — put on this real country-boy voice. Well, he had been a country boy, but this was really exaggerated. He sounded like Andy Griffith on those old re-runs.

"Dad, I heard you tell Aunt Edie and Uncle Robert I might be coming to live with you."

"Well now, that's one of the things we're gonna talk about before this trip is over."

"You mention it to them before you say one word to me!" "To me" came out in a wild, angry squeak. He threw another stone on the fire, a bigger one this time.

"Don't do that, Son," his father said. He sighed. "It just came up in conversation. They wanted to know how you were doin' in school, how your Mama was, things like that. I just mentioned it as a possibility, that's all."

"Yeah — and not one word to me."

"All right, I apologize. I guess I was waitin' for the right moment, some romantic nonsense about us out in a canoe or sittin' around the campfire after cookin' our own fresh-caught fish. I'd bring it up, paint myself in an extremely favourable light, how much fun we'd have and so on and so forth."

Josh looked hard at his father, and smiled. "You don't need to paint yourself in a favourable light."

"No?"

"No."

Charlie doffed an imaginary Stetson. "Why, thank

you.'' Another long drag. Inhale, hold it, hnhh, hnhh, hnhh. Ribet, ribet.

"Would you like to come and live with me Josh?"

Ribet, ribet. Josh's mom had a T-shirt which said, "You have to kiss a lot of frogs before you meet a prince." She and her friends went out with men, but they said nasty things about what they called men-in-general. He knew his mother hoped he wouldn't grow up to be a man-in-general. Men in gen said they believed in equality for women, but they didn't really. Sometimes his mom's friends were really crude and told the kind of jokes about men that the older boys told about girls. One friend in particular, Hedda, told these jokes. And she always called Josh "that little chauvinist piglet." Last week he heard her say to his mother, "Hey, Marie. What's the real reason we still need men?" His mother sounded tired. She was a nurse and the nurses were on strike. She'd just been on a picket line for hours, walking up and down in front of the VGH. "I don't know Hedda, you tell me." "A vibrator can't take out the trash." Hedda always laughed loudly at her own jokes. Josh was glad when his mother said, in a loud, tired, voice, "Very funny."

Charlie had met his mother when he'd crashed his motorcycle and ended up with a broken leg. Compound fractures of the tibia and a dislocated shoulder. When Josh was a little kid his mother taught him the names of all the bones in the body, where they were and what they did. But he didn't like to think about it too much, all that stuff underneath the skin. His mother hadn't been too pleased about the motorcycle trip — still the same old Harley — but Josh had pleaded with her and Charlie had promised he'd be really careful.

His mom said Charlie had probably been reading *Zen and the Art of Motorcycle Maintenance*, and wanted a similar experience with his son. But she finally said okay and gave Josh twenty-five dollars, U.S., to spend however he liked, no questions asked. The trip had been fun and Josh got over being nervous by the second day. Now they were on their way back home. Would he like to come and live with Charlie? He didn't know. Might as well be honest. "I don't know." And then, to change the subject, and because he really wanted to know . . .

"Dad, could you teach me how to wave — so people wave back at me — the way they do to you?"

His father laughed. "I saw you were practising your wavin' all day."

"They all wave at you."

"Well now they don't all wave at me."

"A lot of them do."

"Well, maybe." Hnhh, hnhh, hnhh. "But I really don't have a special signal to get bikers and truckers to wave at me, you know. I mean you tried all kinds of wavin' today and sometimes the bikers and truckers waved at you and sometimes they didn't."

He laughed again. "I hope it doesn't take you as many years as it's taken me to learn I don't make people do things. My wavin' at the bikers and truckers is only one of the variables involved. The guy who doesn't wave may be thinkin' about where he's gonna spend the night, or how much longer he can go before he takes a piss, and the guy who does wave, well — maybe he likes to feel generous or waves at everybody, like the Queen of England. Or just got laid and is feelin' good. Who knows? But I tell you one thing."

"What's that?"

Charlie stretched and smiled at his son. "Motorcycle ridin' seems to be good for sortin' things out."

"What kind of things?"

"Why, any old thing." He put a few more sticks on the fire and the light flared up again. Now the rest of the world was very dark. There was no moon and some high cloud hid the stars.

"Hey, do you mind if I try out a few of my ideas on

you?'' Josh laughed. He was cold now, but he wanted to stay here by his father, by the fire.

''Go ahead,'' he said. ''Sometimes I can't follow you though.''

Now Charlie chuckled. ''That's what my students say.'' Charlie was a research chemist and he also taught at the university. ''Anyway, I'll just toss out a few of the things I've been thinkin' about all day while you've been practising your wavin'. They have to do with motorcycle ridin' and Grandma Sorenson.''

''Grandma Sorenson!'' Josh didn't want to talk about the visit to his grandmother, a very old lady who lived on the family farm in Montana. Grandma Sorenson was senile. The skin on her hands and arms was so thin and white you could see all her veins — like blue worms crawling up and down. It made him feel sick when Charlie suggested he kiss her. His aunt had tied a pink ribbon in her mother's hair. What hair was left. ''Dad,'' Josh said, ''she didn't even recognize us! I can understand she might not recognize me, but she didn't recognize *you*.''

''Hey, hold on. What makes you so sure she didn't recognize us. Now hold your horses.''

''We were standing right there, right by her bed, and she starts talking about her son up in Canada and how his son doesn't live with him and so on.''

''Okay, I admit it's pretty disconcerting. But don't you think it's pretty interesting how we arrive and Aunt Edie says, 'Mother, here's some visitors for you.' The way she opens her eyes and immediately starts talkin' about us?''

''But she was talking about us as though we weren't there! And we were there — right there in front of her.'' He imitated his grandmother's high, thin, grieving voice: ''One of the boys lives up there in Canada. He's a college professor up there. It rains a lot up there in Canada. What's your name?''

There were rustlings in the bushes down by the creek.

Something had come down there to drink. A deer maybe. Not a bear anyway — this wasn't bear country. When he and his mom and Charlie used to go camping in bear country they had to burn up any scraps of food and hang their supplies in a metal box in a tree. Whatever it was down there wasn't going to hurt them. A bear could claw right through a tent. Josh shivered.

"It gave me the creeps."

"Didn't give her the creeps. What she said seemed to make sense to her."

"Even when you told her your name, and my name, she didn't recognize us. How do you explain that?"

His father was irritated but still spoke in his smoky, tolerant voice. "Just at the minute I don't explain it. But I'm workin' on it. And the fact she didn't use your name or my name the whole time we were there doesn't necessarily mean she didn't recognize us."

Josh was tired of this conversation. He blew a few notes on his kazoo. Would the deer wonder what kind of animal that was? "Oh no," he said sarcastically, "not *necessarily*."

"Now don't always take the easy explanation, Josh! If you want to get the most out of the brains you were so obviously born with, you've got to poke, you've got to challenge, you've got to rock the damn boat! I want to know a lot more about the brain," he said, more to himself than to Josh. Josh knew from his father's voice that he didn't have to listen any more. Which was just as well as he was suddenly terribly sleepy. His head kept falling down on his chest and he'd have to jerk it back up.

"I want to know what really gets 'stroked' when you have a stroke," his father said from across the fire. "You know, Josh, everybody who's seen Grandma Sorenson says that she's really in bad shape, she's really mixed up mentally, and that's what I would have thought too, from all the letters people have written me, people who didn't move away like me, people who've known her all their lives, until I saw her the other day. Now I'm not so sure. Maybe she's just usin' language, usin' memory, in a way I haven't thought about before. I think I might be onto somethin' important about the way brains work.''

Josh roused himself one last time. He was flattered that Charlie would try out ideas on him. His mom still treated him like a kid in the idea department. If only he wasn't so sleepy.

''Where do the motorcycles come in?'' he said.

''Well, that's what's really interestin', you see. There's somethin' powerfully paradoxical about ridin' a motorcycle on a trip, not just the real interestin' thing that because I'm up in front and you're hangin' on behind and we've both got our helmets on, so there's no chit-chat like there'd be if we were in a car or a bus and yet our bodies are close, you've got your arms around me for part of the day and it feels good, feels natural — but there's a whole different kind of reality goin' on. Somethin' about payin' close attention to the business of stayin' on the road. But goin' fast on windin' roads like we've been on requires close attention, the margin for error is so small. At sixty miles an hour through a corner, it might be only a couple of inches wide on some corners. Adding a few more miles an hour through that corner might cut the groove down by half or more.''

His father's boyish, excited voice came to him now from very far away. ''You've got to pay attention!'' Josh thought his father was talking to him and forced his eyes open one last time. He wished Charlie would shut up for tonight, but no such luck.

''You've got to pay attention to the drivin'! But the paradox is that payin' such close attention to drivin' seems to stir up and integrate a whole lot of other things. I have more insights and ideas ridin' that motorcycle than I have in a month at the lab or behind my desk back home.'' Josh gave up any pretence of being wide awake and eager for more of his father's insights. He fell asleep as his father said, "Doesn't work that way on the freeway though. I think most of us spend our whole lives on the freeway."

When Josh began to snore Charlie brought himself out of his monologue. "Have you lost it, old son? I don't blame you." The boy was on his side with one arm stretched out towards his father. "I talk too much," Charlie said to the fire. "I just start and keep on going. Asshole," he said to himself. "Jerk." He tried to pick up his son to get him to the tent. "Josh, hey . . . Josh. Hey son, you've got to wake up and crawl into the tent. You've become too big, too big to carry."

"I'm fine," Josh muttered. "Leave me alone. I'm all right here." Why wouldn't this man stop bugging him?

"Now come on!"

"Just leave me here — let me sleep."

He knew it was his father talking to him down through the layers of sleep and darkness but his body refused to move. He felt as though he had dissolved somehow and become part of the very ground he was lying on. His father was making impossible demands. Couldn't he see what had happened?

"Leave me alone." At least that's what he tried to say. It came out as a sort of snarl. Something big was pushing him, dragging him. He didn't care what it was — father, bear, the night itself, so long as it let him sleep.

Charlie laughed as he pulled off Josh's shoes and pants and zipped him into his sleeping bag. "Well," he said, "I knew I was boring, but I didn't know I was that boring!" He closed up the tent and went back out to the fire. He was too wired to sleep just yet, but he liked the idea of Josh curled up there inside the tent, dreaming of god knows what — was he old enough to dream of sex? He wondered idly if Marie had talked to Josh about sex. She was a bit of a prude for someone whose profession was nursing. It was what had originally turned him on. She would wash his back and his chest and then hand him the soapy washcloth so he could do his own privates. She was ten years younger than he was, at least, hardly more than a girl. She must have been about twelve when he dropped his first acid.

"You do it," he said in a weak voice, "sitting up still makes me awful dizzy." She continued to hold out the washcloth. "I don't believe you," she said. But smiled.

They had five good years before it all turned sour. He knew she blamed him, but there were two sides to every story. At least two, he thought, as he built up the fire again and picked up his journal.

Josh saw the sign for the restaurant first. He shouted at his father's back. "Dad, hey Dad, there's the sign!" Charlie slowed down.

"Okay, I see it, keep your shirt on." They turned into the gravel parking in front of a small clapboard building. There were a couple of pick-up trucks outside and a dusty blue van. It was still pretty early in the morning. "Rose's Café," said the hand-painted sign. They'd stopped there for pie à la mode the afternoon before.

Charlie pulled off his helmet. Josh noticed he was already into his Andy Griffith voice. "Boy, I don't know about you but Ah'm hungry."

As they went up the wooden steps Josh said, embarrassed, "Sorry I fell asleep on you last night." He'd been glad when he woke up to see that his father hadn't completely undressed him. Somehow, although he didn't mind jumping into the creek stark naked, he didn't like the idea of Charlie looking at him naked while he was asleep. He'd just started to get some pubic hair.

"Hey, that's perfectly all right. I ended up fallin' asleep on myself. Woke up in the middle of the night with the fire out, a very cold writing hand, my glasses still on and slobber droolin' out of my mouth." He put an arm around Josh's shoulders as they went in and the screen door hissed shut behind them. The restaurant was really old-fashioned, with a counter and booths with padded seats. The early-morning customers were all men. Some of them were kidding the waitress, who had dyed red hair. Two men in a booth were having a conversation about the weather. "And that flash flood," one said, "it just never materialized. I got up in the middle of the night to put the horses away and nothin' happened. We're gonna get it though. Maybe tonight, maybe tomorrow mornin', but it's comin."

Josh turned to his father. "I gotta go to the john."

"Okay, I'll just peel off a few layers of clothing and order. What'd you want?"

"I dunno. Pancakes, I guess." He put his jacket on the seat across from Charlie just as the waitress arrived.

"Hi there, do you want menus or just coffee?" She had a big bright early-morning smile. "Oh," she said, "you boys were in here yesterday." His father laughed, delighted she had remembered. Women liked Charlie. He wasn't exactly handsome, but he had curly hair and a big smile too and a lot of confidence. Lately he'd taken to pumping iron and you could see the muscles underneath his T-shirt.

"That's right," he said, "but the weather looked so threatening and the clouds were building up so fast, we high-tailed it back to Lonesome Creek where we got in some swimmin' and a good night's sleep." "So," he said, looking around and stretching, "Rose's Café, huh? Are you Rose?" She laughed.

"Never was any Rose that I know of. It's our provincial flower. My name's Margie, with a hard *g*."

"Oh. Well, I'm Charlie and the boy on his way to the old boy's room is m'son, Josh."

He wished his father didn't talk quite so loud. He could hear him even after he went through the swinging doors by the kitchen to find the washrooms. "Heifers," said one, and "Steers" the other. "Well, Margie with the hard *g*," said his father's voice, "we *do* want breakfast but

we *don't* need menus; we know what we want. We'll have
a large orange juice, steak . . ." Josh shut the door. "We
aim to please," it said over the urinal. "You aim too,
please." Sometimes it seemed to Josh that grown-ups joked about sex and toilets and stuff like that even more than
kids did. His father was out there ordering steak and all
kind of macho stuff just to impress that waitress. Next
thing you know he'd offer her a ride on the Harley. His
father always had lots of women hanging around him but
when he got drunk or stoned he always called up Marie
and asked if she'd reconsider.

When Josh got back to the booth the juice and coffee
were already on the table. "Did you order me
pancakes?"

"Hotcakes. Margie's corrected me. They call them
hotcakes out here. Yep, buttermilk hotcakes with
blueberry syrup. Sound good?"

"Yeah." His father smiled at him.

"That stuff I was goin' on about last night; did it make
any sense?"

"Which stuff?"

"The stuff about Grandma Sorenson." Josh shook his
head.

"I think I fell asleep too early on." He took a large
swig of juice. Now or never. "Dad — does Mom know
about me maybe going to live with you?"

"She knows," Charlie said. "I wrote her a letter about
it. If she read the letter she knows."

"She hasn't written back or called or anything?"

"Well, I wrote just before we left. I wanted her to have
time to think, maybe talk out loud to herself and say a few
things she wouldn't want you to hear."

"Things about you?"

"Maybe." Josh felt a little tingle of power.

"She doesn't like you."

"I know that."

"She really doesn't like you."

"I know that too." His father's face was quite red. Josh hadn't realized until this moment, watching his father's face, just how much power he had over this man.

"Do you remember," Charlie said, "me talkin' about motorcycles and grooves?"

"A little bit." It was wonderful, this new power he had. He decided to change the subject.

"Dad, can I drive today?"

"Maybe — on a side road. Oh — sure you can. Then you'd find out about the groove. Anyway, you know how we say things are 'groovy' or 'in the groove'?"

"Maybe *you* do," Josh said. Charlie laughed.

"Okay, okay. But jazz musicians say it, and we all said it in the sixties — 'groovin' on the sunshine,' things like that? Well, it all fits together."

"Sorry, you've lost me. What fits together?"

"Well, the basic idea is that there's a groove for me to follow that's exactly right for me to live in, in an optimum way. Guidin' that motorcycle down the groove through a corner has become a metaphor for living in a tuned-in, turned-on way, responsive to things as they come and yet selective. . . ."

"Here you go. Enjoy your breakfast." Margie put the steak and home-fries in front of Josh and laughed flirtatiously at Charlie when he told her to just slide that steak right over here, he needed that red meat. Charlie loved women, especially ordinary women. He'd been ordinary once himself.

"Now, where was I?" Charlie said, picking up his knife and fork. "Oh yeah, and Grandma Sorenson, she's in the gr —"

The man was just there, suddenly, a grey-faced man in a dirty apron. When Josh was little his mom would sometimes give him left-over bits of dough to play with. Eventually, if he rolled out and kneaded and punched them around too long, they turned grey coloured — the colour of this man. He stood there by the booth and just broke right into the middle of Charlie's sentence.

"You fellas didn't get as far as you wanted to yesterday." The man's voice was flat, like the voice of the psychopathic killers on TV.

"Oh," Charlie said, "hi there. No, we got worried about the weather and decided to go back and camp at Lonesome Creek. Came back here for breakfast though. Sure is a good place to eat."

"You think so?" said the man in a flat tone of disbelief. Josh didn't like this guy standing there by his shoulder while he tried to eat his breakfast.

"Hey Dad," he said, deliberately ignoring the man. "Can I have some money for the juke-box?" There was a small juke-box selector at every booth.

"Are you out of money already?" Charlie reached into his pocket but the weirdo was quicker.

"Here," he said, tossing two quarters on the table, "play Anne Murray. I like to listen to her. C-3."

"I don't . . ." Josh looked at his father in desperation.

"Go on," Charlie said, "play Anne Murray and then you can choose the next one." Josh put in one quarter and waited. Soon they heard Buddy Holly singing "Peggy Sue."

"That's not Anne Murray," the man said. He leaned across Josh and pointed. "Hah, it says right here, C-3. 'Snowbird.' Anne Murray."

"My finger must have slipped," Josh said. The man stank of sweat and something else.

"Here's your quarter back," Josh said.

"Don't matter."

The man in the other booth, the one who had been talking about horses and flash floods, yelled out, "Hey Margie, bring me a fresh cup of coffee, will ya, and one of them jelly doughnuts."

"Coming right up."

"They shouldn't serve people like that," the grey man said. Charlie smiled.

"People who ask for fresh cups of coffee and jelly doughnuts?"

"Murderers," the man said. "People who murder other people." He looked at Charlie and seemed to be trying to make up his mind about something.

"Do you mind if I sit down?"

"Well, no," Charlie said, "we've got to hit the road pretty soon, but I don't mind."

"Dad," Josh whispered, "I don't want him sitting here!"

"It's okay Josh. Really."

"It's not okay. *Really*."

Charlie wasn't pleased that Marie had made Josh so uptight about strangers or anybody different.

The man slid in next to Josh and shoved the juice away. "You see," he said, "I've got the brain of a little girl who died. That man over there — that Kolozoff — he killed her."

"Dad!"

Charlie was staring at the man. "You've got the brain of a little girl who died?"

"That's right." He swallowed hard. "The doctors said I had somethin' wrong with my brain and I'd have to see a specialist, I got epilepsy." He turned to Josh.

"You know what that is? Epilepsy?"

"Sort of," Josh said. "Dad — I —" Josh was afraid he was going to be sick. The man's hands were bitten way down past the white part of the nail. Gross. "I'm going to play another Buddy Holly," Josh said. "I like those songs. I'll use my own quarter." Anything to drown out the sound of this man's voice.

"They say I'm crazy and maybe I am, but I know something that they don't know."

"Oh, really," said Charlie, "what's that?" Margie appeared with the coffee pot. How could his father sit there chewing on steak while this nutcase was talking all this crazy talk.

"Earl," Margie said, "Harry wants you in the kitchen." She poured Charlie another cup of coffee. The man gave her a look of contempt.

"Tell Harry I'll be there in a minute."

"He wants you right now, Earl." To Charlie, "Is he bothering you?"

"Not at all," Charlie said, "I'm really interested in what he has to say. I'm very interested in the brain."

"Say," the man was getting excited now. "Are you a doctor?" Maybe he was going to have a fit. Sometimes they frothed at the mouth and bit their tongues. Josh had never seen a fit but he'd heard about them. He really thought he was going to throw up any minute.

"Not the kind you mean," Charlie said, "but I am interested in the brain."

"Well, they sent me over to Calgary, see," the man said, "and laid me on a table and put something over my face while they stuck needles in my head. But just before they covered up my face, I saw a little girl on a stretcher, across the room, a pretty little girl of about five or six and later, while I was laying there I could feel her brain comin' in — or the mind part of it anyway. At least the nerve section. Ever since then, I've had this vision, or her dream or her memory. Anyhow — it's the same thing over and over. Just like I was there in that little girl's body. She was on a wheat combine. She'd ridden her pony out to it with two other kids. I can see their bodies but their faces are blanks — like they'd been erased or something."

"Dad," Josh said, "let's go."

"Finish your breakfast, Son."

"Oh, let him go," the man said. "Kids these days don't want to know nothin."

"No," Charlie said, "I'd like him to stay."

"I'm finished," Josh said, "I don't want any more breakfast. I'll see you outside." He almost pushed the man onto the floor in his eagerness to escape.

"I could feel her mind," the man was saying, "comin' in and I just said to my own brain, 'brain, KEEP . . . STILL.' And her memory or whatever, came on in just like it had been there forever. I saw her tie the reins to the wheat combine and I saw Kolozoff —" Josh slammed the screen door hard. Margie came after him.

"Don't mind Earl," she said, "he's harmless."

"What's he talking about then, brains and dead little girls?"

"Oh, he's got a bee in his bonnet about Larry Kolozoff — thinks he killed some little girl by whipping her horse and dragging her across a field."

"Was there a dead little girl?"

Margie laughed. "Sure, and her name was Rose." She took an Oh Henry bar out of her pocket. "You're goin' to be hungry without that breakfast."

"I'll be okay."

"Shall I bring you out some pie?"

"No, no thanks. But could you tell my dad to hurry?"

"Sure thing."

Josh wishes he knew how to drive the Harley. What he'd really like to do is take off and leave Charlie stranded there. Instead he sits on the porch steps and eats the candy bar and tries not to think about the grey man — Earl — and his bitten fingers. When Charlie appears, Josh puts on his helmet and says nothing until they're both seated on the motorcycle and about to go. "You know what Mom says?" he shouts. "She says you never listen to anybody. She says you've got elephantitis of the ego! That's what Mom says." At this, Charlie turns around in his seat.

"Now I know you're feelin' a bit fed up with me just now Josh, but let's leave your mother out of it, shall we?" He revs the engine.

"If you wanna fight, let's fight fair."

"Just go!" Josh screams at him. "Just get going! I'd never live with you."

"We'll talk about it later."

"I don't want to talk about it later! My decision's final."

"So you say." They move out of the parking lot and onto the highway, spraying gravel as they go.

Breeders

Breeders

After Corinne fainted in the Picasso museum and everyone was so horrible to her — well not exactly horrible but they stuck her upstairs where the photo exhibit was, the only part of the museum that was *climatisé*, and kept talking at her in French, should they call a doctor? *les pompiers?* and they couldn't find Jeff, even though she described him exactly and told them about his T-shirt which said "The Gang of Four" — she got really freaked out and decided she would go and visit her brother Fred, who was with the embassy in Copenhagen.

She had been up on the top floor for about half an hour, alone most of the time and when she came down Jeff was sitting out in the courtyard with their college friend Martine, drinking orange juice and chatting. He hadn't even missed her, hadn't even known she was sick. They never walked around museums tied together, he said, so how was he to know she was in trouble? Jeff didn't know she was pregnant, but Martine did, and offered to take a cab back to the place where they were staying on the rue Monge. From the impatient look on Jeff's face Corinne knew it was all over between them and that he had wanted to spend this afternoon in the company of Martine. He would say it was because Martine was bilingual and really knew her way around — he always had good reasons. Corinne knew she'd better start to make other plans. She got Martine to entice Jeff out to a movie while she packed up some stuff, wrote a note and got herself over to the Gare du Nord. She'd be back, but right now she needed some pampering and a change of scene.

It wasn't that she expected her brother to solve her problems for her — Martine could probably do that — but she suddenly wanted to see family, especially Fred, the black sheep. If her parents found out what had happened to her she'd be a black sheep as well — two black sheep in a family of white sheep, spotless sheep really. Her mother would say to her father, "Now what have we done to deserve *this*?" She might add, pushing her hair back behind her ear and giving a little smile, "At least Corinne's *normal*; what she's done is silly but at least it's *normal*."

"I guess I'm like your grandfather," she said to Corinne once, "I really don't like anything abnormal. Remember how he always had to have housekeepers who were attractive? He couldn't stand to be around anything ugly."

"You don't think it's abnormal to choose a housekeeper by her looks and not by how well she can keep a house? I find *that* abnormal." Corinne was at what her mother called the argumentative stage. Grandfather, before he died, employed a series of stunningly beautiful housekeepers, none of whom could cook worth a damn. He even bought paper plates by the hundreds so they wouldn't have to do so much washing up. They sat up front with him, in his old Buick, when he went shopping while the dust kittens gathered under furniture. But he didn't marry any of them and he left his money to his children, so Corinne supposed that all that other stuff was abnormal in a normal sort of way. She hadn't minded the housekeepers but she hated going there for Sunday dinner and cutting up food on a paper plate.

She sat up all night on the Viking Express and was very glad to see Fred waiting at the Central Station. All around her, college kids like herself had been chatting and flirting and exchanging information about cheap hotels and hostels, places to eat. She felt sad and worldly wise, set apart from them by her secret sorrow. She read a Jean Rhys novel, lent to her by Martine, and dozed.

The train went right on the ferry and was held down with huge chains. Most people headed right for the Duty Free Shop. Corinne wandered through but didn't see anything she really wanted to buy. Fred got a booze allowance from the Embassy and she couldn't imagine bringing him a box of fancy chocolates. A girl who looked Danish was buying bag after bag of liquorice all-sorts. It seemed a funny thing to spend your money on.

In the Picasso museum there had been lots of sculptures and paintings of pregnant women that the artist had done when he was about to become a father again at the age of sixty-seven. Some of her friends' parents were divorced and the fathers married again to much younger women who wanted babies. That was natural. Men could have babies pretty well up to the day they died. There was that cellist, the Spanish one. He was eighty or something and had a baby. She wondered if her grandfather had ever slept with any of those housekeepers.

She hadn't fainted because of all those pregnant women; she had fainted because the museum was so hot and stuffy and because she had thrown up her breakfast before they set out. The lights in the hall and in the toilets at their hotel only stayed on for two minutes. She stood over the toilet bowl, in the sudden darkness, retching. Maybe it would be better to have the abortion done in Denmark than in France. France was a Catholic country and she was also under age — at least back home in Massachusetts. They'd probably want her parents' consent. And her mother would want her to keep the baby, she just knew it. After Fred defected (that's what they called it between themselves, "Fred's defection") her mother said, "Well, it's up to you Corinne, to make me a grandmother." Martine had an abortion — she said it didn't hurt. But they'd seen *Dirty Dancing* last month and Lisa nearly died in that — the sheets were covered in blood.

Fred brought his current boyfriend to the station. (This is my friend Äse — my friend Awser — at first Corinne thought he was trying to be funny.) Äse picked up her bag and as they moved away she could see that Fred was limping badly. "Two broken toes," her brother said. "In pursuit of knowledge. It was Selena's fault really. She had taken it into her head to dust — as some final gesture — hoping for a bigger wedding present perhaps." Selena was Fred's Hong Kong maid whom he had brought with him to Copenhagen. Now she had decided to get married to a Danish widower and Fred found the whole thing very funny. He had written Corinne a letter about it. "In any event," he said, "her zeal evaporated, or maybe one of her friends rang up, before she put things back in the study. Or before she had replaced *The Encyclopedia Britannica*. I came home late and didn't notice, so when I got up in the night and went into the study to make some notes, wham bam thank you ma'am I went flying."

"He went into work the next day," Äse said, "but his foot was turning purple with little streaks of purple up the leg. When he fainted, they sent him to hospital."

"You fainted," Corinne said, "what day was that?"

"I don't remember, about a week ago, why?"

"Nothing," she said, "no reason. I'll need to change some money."

"I am very impressed that you travel so lightly," Äse said. "Most of the young people one sees are carrying these enormous packs. I always think of them as life-support systems — like the men carry on the moon."

"Oh they are, they are," Fred said. "They contain large quantities of clean underwear with one's name sewn in on Cash's name tapes, and socks and deodorant and chocolate bars and Wrigley's gum to distribute to urchins. Soap. Deodorant. Toilet paper. Americans cannot travel without these things and they are afraid that Europe may not feel quite the same about personal hygiene as they do. There may be *shortages.*"

"I left most of my stuff in Paris," Corinne said, counting her money and putting it away before she left the *Change* wicket. "With a friend."

"A friend, a friend," said Äse. "When one speaks of 'a friend' and gives no name that usually means a friend of the opposite sex. Or that's what it usually means with girls." He smiled ("This is my friend Awser," and in Hong Kong my friend Jimmy, in Delhi my friend Ranjan, in London my friend Michael. Sooner or later Fred had always found a "friend.")

Fred opened the door of a taxi. "We're going to the races this afternoon. Do you want to go home first and freshen up or would you like to have a long leisurely lunch downtown and then proceed directly to the *Galopbane*?"

"I've never been to a horse-race," Corinne said, "but I'd like to take a bath and wash my hair first. If that's okay. If there's time?"

"You see," said Fred, after giving the taxi driver directions, "personal hygiene wins out over *koldt bord* and good Danish beer." He got in beside her and patted her knee in a brotherly fashion.

"Never mind, we do understand. Sitting up all night is not much fun. We'll have some fruit and cheese at home and a meal later on, after the races. We have become addicted to the races at the *Galopbane*. It's very small, very pretty – reminds me a bit of New England.''

"Do you win?'' Corinne said.

"When he wins,'' Äse said, "he wins all afternoon. Last week he lost all afternoon. It evens up.'' Äse was very good looking, with curly dark-blond hair and bright blue eyes. Corinne wasn't sure what men looked for in other men but by her standards he was certainly handsome. His hair was receding a little bit at the temples, as was Fred's, and he wasn't a poster Dane but he was enormously attractive. He too worked for the Embassy, he said, as a translator and liaison officer.

The house was very pretty, ochre-coloured stucco with a large garden at the back and a formal hedge in front. Corinne was surprised that Fred was not living in an apartment of some sort.

"Everyone before me has been married with at least one kid. I think they want to hold on to the place which is nice for me, except it means I have to put up with every cultural visitor who comes through — unless they are very very big. Actually, it's kind of fun. Opera singers singing in the shower, jazz musicians and minor poets smoking up on the veranda, painters making appreciative noises about the light.''

"Do they have to eat Selena's cooking?'' Selena was the worst cook Corinne had ever experienced. If it weren't that she was also extremely plain it might be thought that Fred was following in his maternal grandfather's footsteps. When Corinne went out to visit Fred in Hong Kong she was served canned chili and hot dogs and desserts like orange Jello, meals like that in a city of gourmet delights. Fred said she had worked for an American family for five years and the children would eat nothing but the most banal American food. Now it was all she would cook. Fred liked good food. Corinne couldn't understand why he dragged Selena around with him. Maybe she was very discreet about his sexual habits.

The one thing she did well was garden, and the garden at the back of the house was beautiful.

"I take the visitors to restaurants," Fred said. "I wouldn't waste a jar of Cheez Whiz on strangers. It will be hard to find a replacement of her calibre."

Äse came in from the kitchen with three bottles of beer and some cheese and flatbread.

"Rest your leg," he said to Fred, "I'll show her where she is to sleep." She followed him up the stairs. He opened a door to the right, which revealed a small corridor and then another door. "It's strange, isn't it? Perhaps this is where they kept the old mother. At any rate, you will be very private."

He put her case down on a luggage stand. This was obviously a room, now, for visitors. They could be private, yes, but so could Fred. Fred and a friend. She wondered if Äse actually lived here — would that be allowed, these days? He was tall, like her brother, but well built, heavier.

"Thank you for meeting me at the station," Corinne said.

"But of course we would meet you. Fred has been very happy ever since he got your call."

"Really?" Corinne was pleased.

"Really, really. Now you have about ten minutes, fifteen at the most. He will *not* be happy if we miss the first race. I'll put your food and drink on the bureau here. There's a hair-dryer in the bathroom." He went out and shut the door.

The soap in the shower was Imperial Leather, which she didn't like, but she was already wet when she reached for it. As she washed herself she thought about her brother. He was thirteen years older and yet had never been impatient or dismissive with her as a child. She could only remember him shouting at her once, when she was about four. She had wandered upstairs and into the bathroom which he had forgotten to lock. He was just getting out of the shower and was naked, with what she later knew was a huge hard-on. She had never seen a man naked before, and with this huge *thing*.

"Don't you ever knock!" he had screamed at her, red-faced and furious. "Get out!"

She backed away and heard the door slam behind her, the bolt shoot home. And did not go howling to her mother. She must have felt she was in the wrong, not Fred. Years later she wondered if maybe the hot water had given him an erection and he had been shy, not angry because he was about to jerk himself off. He never apologized but he was very gentle with her for the rest of his school holidays.

His pubic hair was red. She was dark, like her mother; it was her father and brother who had the red hair, although her father's was white now and Fred's had faded.

What did he and Åse do with one another? Weren't they afraid of AIDS? Denmark was supposed to be very liberal. Was there a lot of AIDS here? She had seen magazine pictures of young men dying of AIDS. They both looked very fit, tall, healthy men in the prime of life. But one of them could be carrying it. Anybody could be carrying it. Suppose she had an abortion and haemorrhaged? She might be given AIDS-infected blood. It had happened to people with haemophilia, and a woman in Canada had died three years after a blood transfusion. It made her feel faint just to think about it. Whichever way she thought about it — having the baby or having the abortion — it made her feel sick. Would she be able to bring up the subject if Åse were always around?

On the shelf with the hair-dryer, in the bathroom, was one of those stupid My Little Pony dolls. This one was pink with bleached-blonde hair. It must have been left by the last family and Fred had kept it as a joke. Or maybe Åse had given it to him because he liked going to the races. It looked silly next to the shaving mug and shaving brush and razor. The little kids went crazy over them.

Her friend Julie's half-sister owned about a dozen and liked to comb their manes and talk to them. Better than Rambo and G.I. Joe but pretty useless.

The mane was coarse — a real horse's mane might feel like that. Some of her friends had horses but Corinne had never touched one, let alone sat on one. Theirs was not a horsey family. When had Fred acquired this passion for the races? Maybe at the same time as he made friends with Äse. Girls did that kind of thing all the time — learned to like what their boyfriends liked. It hardly ever worked the other way around.

"Are you enjoying yourself?" Äse smiled at her. Corinne smiled back. "Oh yes. It's not at all as I imagined it. Fred's right — it's like some country scene back home. People sauntering around, babies, kids. It's charming."

Corinne had seen twins in a double pushchair and bet on "Gemini" in the third race. She won twenty-seven kroner on a ten-kroner bet and was very pleased with herself. Fred had not won anything yet, nor Äse.

"Most of the women I know rely on intuition when they bet," he said. They were sitting on white chairs in the covered grandstand, eating hot dogs with *brod*. Corinne realized that for the first time in weeks she was having fun. It had something to do with the sunny afternoon and the excitement of betting on a horse-race and of course to do also with the certain knowledge that if she asked him, Fred would help her. But it had to do with Äse as well — she realized she was turned on by Äse, by his merry face and his courtesy and the way he had included her in the phrase "most of the women I know." She and Jeff had been together since grade twelve. He probably never thought of her as a woman.

Galumpf, Galumpf, Galumpf, went the loudspeaker and they played the song that signalled the start of another race. The chairs they were sitting on were numbered and Fred decided to change his seat in order to change his luck. Corinne and Äse remained where they were. Corinne had bet thirty kroner on "Moby Dick" because she was from Massachusetts. The jockey had a white whale on his cap and on his green silk shirt. They had gone down to the paddock to see the horses, now accompanied by stable ponies, circle in front of the grandstand. It was a race for two-year-olds.

"Some say they are too young," Fred told her, "that it's not good for them; but aren't they beautiful!"

Most of the stable-hands were girls of her own age and even younger, but the jockeys looked old, with wrinkled, nut-coloured faces. She didn't like looking at them very much — they reminded her of dwarfs and midgets.

"Of the hundreds of thousands of Thoroughbreds running at any track in the world today," Äse said, "the pedigree of every one of them can be traced back, through the male line, to one of three stallions at stud in late-seventeenth-century England." Corinne smiled. She knew Äse was showing off for her.

"Really?" she said.

"Really."

"Pedigree," Fred said, "that must come from foot, somehow. I should have paid more attention in Latin class."

"When I was a very little boy," Äse said, "my mother and father used to bring me here to Klampenborg to watch the races and sometimes the royal family walked around in the ring. If one is talking about bloodlines, pedigrees, then as a good Dane I should mention that the Danish royal family is the oldest royal dynasty in Europe."

"And if one is talking about *peds*," said Fred, "my foot hurts. Let's make our bets and get something to eat and go and sit down."

Fred came back up to join them after the race. His choices for one and two had both won and he was elated.

"I'll take you somewhere fancy tonight," he said to his

sister, "down by the water. I had bet a lot on that race."

Down by the starting gate a pretty blonde girl, in a pale silk raincoat and holding a cellophane-wrapped bouquet, was being interviewed by a reporter from a television station.

"Is that one of the royal family?" Corinne asked.

"No, I don't think so. The daughter of an owner, maybe." Äse smiled.

"Girls and horses, girls and horses. They go together, don't they?"

"And yet we have the compelling image of the centaur, half man, half horse," said Fred. "I don't think I've ever seen a statue or picture of a female centaur."

"Of course you have," Äse said. "Or you have if you have seen the movie *Fantasia*. Surely you, as Americans, have seen that movie?"

"Äse loves old American films," Fred said, putting his hand on his friend's knee. Äse smiled and looked at the hand. He picked it up and gently gave it back to Fred. Corinne was afraid to look at either of them. She was *really* turned on by that, Fred's long, slim hand, a larger version of her own, on Äse's knee.

"Fred took me to *Fantasia*, when I was little," she said. "I don't remember much about it except I got scared when Zeus or somebody threw thunderbolts."

"And I was stoned," Fred said. "It was in the early seventies, a re-issue. It was quite the thing to get stoned and go and see *Fantasia*. I don't remember a female centaur."

"Oh yes, she was white, with blonde hair. The male centaur had blue hair I think, and it was in the bit with Zeus — the *Pastoral* Symphony, wasn't it?"

"He had to take me out," Corinne said, "I was frightened."

"And there is a Botticelli," Äse said, "in the Uffizi, I think, with a female centaur. She is not the main character; King Midas is the main character. But in the lower right-hand corner a female centaur is suckling her child while a male centaur is bringing her something that looks like a dead squirrel. So there's two. But there aren't many, I don't think. Centaurs are usually male. It is a very old myth.''

"There must have been females," Fred said, "or there would have been no babies.''

"I think the centaurs came from the union of women with horses." He smiled down at the place where Fred's hand had been, then turned to Corinne. "What do you think?" Was he teasing her? Flirting? She stood up.

"Let's go bet again.''

Fred shook his head. "Hooked. One afternoon at the races and she's hooked. All right, let's go look over the horses — they're Arabian this time — and place our bets. After this race maybe we'll go on into town and find a lovely place to eat.''

"Are you coming with us?" Corinne said to Äse.

"With your permission." He smiled and bowed. "Have you seen *The Black Stallion*?"

"Of course.''

"He was an Arabian, *is* an Arabian, although not the most famous or most valuable Arabian in the world. That one is worth about ten million U.S. dollars. The purest stock is in Egypt. You can see paintings of these lovely creatures in Egyptian tombs. The Arabian horse has a closer relationship to man than any other animal except a dog.''

"When his ship comes in," Fred said, "Äse is going to buy an Egyptian-Arabian and live in the desert like a Bedouin.''

"Yes, that would be lovely. No more translating of memos and greetings.''

"But no movies," Corinne said.

"Perhaps I could have a VCR that ran on a small generator in my tent.''

"Äse says the Arabians know the sexual differences between human beings," Fred said. They were leaning against the paddock fence as the horses were being brought out.

"But it's true! When a woman trainer leads the Arabian to serve at stud, the sperm amount is fifteen percent higher than when a man is in control."

Corinne was embarrassed by this talk of studs and sperm counts and she had a feeling Äse knew she was. Could he tell she was pregnant, somehow, or was he just teasing her, trying to see how sophisticated she really was?

A small, dark woman had been listening to them with great interest. Now she addressed Fred.

"Ex-coos me, are you breedish?"

Fred smiled down at her. "No," he said, "we're Americans."

She shook her head. "No, no, breedish — *horse* breedish. Do you breed horses?" Fred managed to keep a straight face.

"I'm afraid not."

The woman smiled, showing several gold teeth, and handed him a magazine. She said they could keep it anyway. It was all about Egyptian-Arabian horses, with photos and descriptions and everything.

As soon as the woman had moved far enough away, they began to laugh.

"Breeders," Fred said, the tears rolling down his face. "Breeders!"

That night Corinne slept badly, with shifting dreams. As soon as she woke up they faded. Something to do with apples, maybe, and a classroom where she had to make a presentation. Finally she got up quietly and made her way down the hall to where Fred and Äse were sleeping. She wrapped a blanket around herself and lay down outside their door. She didn't know what she wanted, exactly, except not to be so far away. Snores came from the other side of the door. Äse? Fred? She didn't know, but she found it strangely comforting.

Trash

Trash

My husband always used to let me choose the tenants for
the upstairs suite. Perhaps ''let'' isn't exactly the right
word as I was perfectly aware of the fact that he didn't
want anything to do with it — the choosing of tenants —
if he could possibly avoid it. That way it was clear from
the beginning that I was the landlady and the rules — no
typing after 11 P.M., no baths or showers before 6 A.M.,
no rowdy parties, rent due and payable on the last day of
each month — were *my* rules, nothing to do with him. He
was just the pleasant if somewhat distant husband of the
landlady, the man who said ''hello'' or ''hello there'' in
passing and changed a fuse if a circuit got overloaded.

''You'll see to it, won't you,'' he would say as the time
drew near for our annual ad in the university rental sheet.
''You see to it, won't you? You do it so well.'' His con-
tribution was cleaning up after the last tenants (another
rule was ''please leave this suite the way you found it''
but nobody ever did and this was the early sixties, long
before the days of damage deposits and the many regula-
tions that now make up the Landlord and Tenant Act).

He mended any of the Sally Ann furniture that needed mending or replaced it with more of the same if it was beyond repair. He washed the walls and painted them if they were too grimy. So he did his share, no doubt about that, but I was always the one who had to deal with the actual people.

We never rented out the upstairs suite for more than ten months: during July and August relatives visited, or friends, and it was nice to have a place to put them where they (and we) could have some privacy. Ours was an old house, just south of Broadway, near Alma, in a shabby genteel district. Not a very interesting house architecturally but large and friendly and from the bathroom in the upstairs suite you got a view of the mountains. The suite was very easy to rent out.

And so, along about the middle of August our name would go in to the university, the telephone would start ringing and I would interview prospective tenants, traipse them up and down the stairs, show them the rules which I had typed neatly and posted on the back of the door — like the rules in a French hotel or pension — and if we all liked each other well enough to enter into a relationship of this sort, they would sign another copy of the rules, give me the first and last months' rent in advance and move in the end of the month.

I had to be strict. I too was a student, doing graduate work, and we had two young children. I studied at night, after the kids were in bed, and for two hours in the early mornings, before everybody woke up. I was also a TA (a teaching assistant) in order to get the money for my fees and a baby-sitter the few hours a week I was actually teaching or in a seminar. I never stayed at the university to study and my social life up there was limited to a coffee at the Graduate Centre if I had an hour between classes. One of the male graduate students once told me he thought I was a very "romantic" figure, the way I kept

appearing and disappearing so mysteriously. I just looked
at him.

So I studied in the kitchen, sometimes falling asleep
right there with my head on a book or a pile of English
100 essays. My husband would eventually miss me and
come wake me up, insisting I go to bed. When I think
back on those years now I see myself as always tired and
grumpy but neither my friends nor my children remember me that way at all. I must have been a better actress
than I thought. I seemed to see the world through a glassy
shimmer, the way you see the landscape near a barbecue
or campfire.

We had a basement suite as well but that was more or
less permanently rented to a tugboat captain who worked
for Kingcome Navigation and was away more than he
was at home. He had a separate entrance (the real
drawback with the upstairs suite was that it shared the
same entrance as we had) and we hardly ever saw him except once in a while along Broadway, always wearing a
grey felt hat. Once he bought the children ice-cream
cones when we happened to meet in *Peter's*. He used to get
a newspaper from the John Howard Society (one of my
other duties as landlady was to sort out all the mail and
deliver it to the tenants or forward it if they'd moved on)
and I never even glanced at it, never knew what it was until one Christmas afternoon, just as we were about to
carve the turkey in front of an admiring group of students
from International House, Cap'n Willis staggered up the
back-porch stairs and asked my husband to take him to
the hospital. He'd been on a three-day bender, drinking
vodka and eating nothing and was seeing things. I was
fascinated by the fact that sick as he was (and he was a terrible colour) he was wearing his grey felt hat. After a few
weeks he reappeared, apologized and vowed it would
never happen again. He was with us for another year
quiet as could be, and then he took a job up in Prince

Rupert. The John Howard Society newsletter came for years (it was the only mail he ever got) but he'd left no forwarding address so I just threw it away.

So, except for that one solitary incident the basement suite had never been a problem but the upstairs suite was another matter altogether. For one thing, it usually involved two people living directly over our heads (one year two Japanese-Canadian sisters, another year a young Canadian in the German department and his new German wife, once two young men from the Vancouver School of Art) and, as I have already mentioned, there was no separate entrance for this suite. We had French doors on the sitting-room (to the left as you came in) and a door on the children's room (to the right) but tenants had to come up the front steps, open the front door and proceed up the stairs to the suite. All this never seemed to bother them but it bothered me. It *really* bothered me. Our house was old and had no insulation whatsoever; every noise carried. I could hardly legislate what time people came in (it had occurred to me to put in the rules "no admittance after 11 P.M." but I knew I couldn't do that, it wouldn't be fair) and so I put up with people knocking over the milk bottles which had been carefully put out for the Dairyland man or calling cheerful, loud good-byes to friends who had dropped them off. The kids woke up and as I was in the kitchen I was the one who went to comfort them: "Shh, shh, it's only John and Trudl, Joe and Simon, Hannah and Allan, shh, shh."

And so our life continued, me studying on the kitchen table, the children growing a little older — one of them now at the Acadia Daycare Centre three mornings a week, an amazing thing for me as daycare was not yet an accepted thing — my husband continuing to ask me to choose the tenants "because you do it so well." I was longing for a study, a room of my own, tired of always having to remove my books from the kitchen table while I cooked or we ate or played games with the children. We had no dining-room; we slept in what had been the dining-room. The shimmering haze through which I viewed the world seemed to be getting worse. I had completed my MA thesis — god knows how — and was studying for my comprehensives. I was also teaching two sections of English 100 and exams were coming up. I was trying to be Super-Mother, never a TV dinner in our house or a cake mix. People said, "I don't know how you do it." I should have paid attention to such remarks but of course I didn't. I was flattered and determined to try harder. But I began to resent my husband's attitude to all this. I kept asking him when when *when* can we stop renting out one of the suites, when can I have a place, a study, a corner for myself? He said soon, soon (in the same tone I used to hush the children, "shh, shh") we can't quite afford it just yet.

And then we decided to go to England for the summer, to see my husband's parents. There was some terrific fare available through the B.C. Teachers' Federation and as our youngest was not quite two, she could go free. Our eldest was born in England but the grandparents had never seen the little one. It was too good an opportunity to pass up. I was to take my comprehensives in June and we would be away for July and August. I wanted to say to him why don't you leave me here and take the children on your own but I couldn't think of a valid reason. My teaching would be over, my comprehensives — presumably — passed. There was no excuse for staying behind. I couldn't bring myself to say, "I want to be alone, I want to *stop* for a while." For when, really, did he stop, when did he have a spell of time to call *his* own? Besides, we would need to rent out the house to help towards the cost of the trip. Deep down I was seething with resentment. The money for the trip would have paid for the upstairs suite to be empty for at least six months. A room — *rooms* — to work in, study in, be alone in. For I was a glutton for punishment; I had enrolled as a candidate for

a Ph.D. And I wanted to spend a summer camping, or
sprawled in our own backyard. Vancouver was lovely in
the summertime, still is. Why go to England and dress up
the children and be polite? But I agreed to it all and even
began making little summer dresses and telling stories
about England, about Grannie and Grandpa, instead of
the usual bedtime stories. And I knew how much my husband's parents missed him; they hadn't seen him in five
years.

A teacher from Golden, B.C., arranged to take the entire house — except the basement suite — for July and
August. I was pleased that was settled so easily and I
could get on with my studying. Our most recent tenant
had left a few weeks before the end of April. He was a nice
young man whose girlfriend slept over on the weekends.
The two of them made boisterous love directly over our
sitting-room every Saturday night. We got used to it,
more or less, but it was pretty awful if we had guests. We
would all raise our voices as things got more and more
vocal until we were practically shouting at one another,
and then gradually sink back into normal conversation as
the cries diminished to moans and sighs. My husband
wanted me to speak to him, discreetly, but there I drew
the line. "Speak to him yourself," I said, but he never
did. Sunday mornings I would see them go off hand in
hand to catch the bus to her place, where they spent Sunday nights. He was a graduate student in biology —
something to do with the brains of hummingbirds.

Over dinner one night in early May my husband suggested we rent out the upstairs suite for six weeks, at a
reduced rate — it would be a little extra cash for the trip.
We had a terrific row about that — I had moved my
books to the upstairs kitchen — but somehow he per-
suaded me, he always could. We would leave the children
with his parents and have a slap-up weekend in London
on our own — something like that. I went and retrieved
my books and papers and brought them all downstairs.

Then I placed an ad in the *Sun* for three days and waited. Who would want a suite for only six weeks? I hoped no one would answer and on the first day no one did. The second day several people came but either they wanted to negotiate a longer rental or I didn't like their looks and quickly thought of new rules (no smoking, no overnight visitors). In one instance I told the people that we were vegetarians and couldn't possibly rent to anyone who cooked meat. I was shameless that day in my attempts to keep the suite for myself.

And then, around 4:30 in the afternoon a young couple with a baby knocked on the door. The ad said "no children, no pets" so I was very surprised. I asked them if they had read the ad carefully and they said yes, but they'd driven all the way from Calgary and were desperate for a place to stay. Just for six weeks. They had a cousin in Burnaby who had promised they could move in with her on July 1st. The husband — Danny — had been offered a temporary job as an emcee in a nightclub downtown. He was "in the entertainment business" but this was the first work he'd found in months. So they'd packed up and driven all night, but hadn't known how hard it would be to find a place that would take a baby.

They were very young, maybe nineteen (the girl) and twenty (the boy). I wasn't much older myself, twenty-six, but I *felt* older, a woman who had a husband with a steady job, a house with suites, two clean, well-fed children who didn't have to be packed up and driven through the mountains to another city because their father couldn't find a job. I might bitch about lack of space and too much to do but really I had had a pretty nice life so far. I tell you all this because I am trying to explain why, after all my lies and manoeuvres to keep out several prospective tenants who would probably be much more congenial, more reliable, than this bedraggled pair and their baby, I decided to rent to them. Once inside (and after they'd seen the upstairs) the girl kept looking around our sitting-room and saying, "This is sure nice," and smiling at my daughters, who were intrigued by the baby, a sickly look-ing boy of about nine months. I felt *guilty*. I knew it was madness, that I was already operating on a kind of emo-tional overdraft and that I would probably regret it the next day, but I rented to them. I did insist on cash, not a cheque, and a month's rent in advance. When the young man, who was a bit of a swaggerer and darkly good look-ing in a sharp-faced way, mentioned again that he'd be working nights, I got him to promise to wear running shoes going to and from his job. Then I lent them our old crib, a playpen, coffee, milk, sugar and left them to settle in. The suite had been freshly painted and I had put a jug of spring flowers on the kitchen table. "Oh," the girl said to me, "I just know our luck's gonna change in a place like this."

Need I say that my husband thought I'd gone off my head, that we had a strict rule about no children and for a very good reason. I'd have to go up there and tell them there'd been some mistake. "You go," I said, "you tell them." And then, basking in the warm glow of a Good Deed I added, "We have *so much!*"

"Well," he said, "it's up to you of course; you're the one with exams coming up. I just hope you don't regret it."

And it was all right for the first ten days or so. The girl, Margie, was the one I saw most. I let her use our washing machine and she came down every other day with a load of soiled clothes, mostly baby clothes, and washed them while the baby had his nap, or put him on a blanket in the garden if he were awake. She had her own clothes-pegs with her, the ends marked with bright red nail polish so her pegs wouldn't get mixed up with mine. She was a pale, long-legged girl, taller than her husband, with frizzy brown hair. If the weather were nice she sometimes sat in the backyard and read a movie magazine while the clothes were doing. She told me the baby's name was Paladin because she'd been watching that program when her pains began and besides she thought Richard Boone was really sexy. She was surprised that we didn't have a TV and didn't allow one in the suite. She said they sold their TV and all their furniture before they left Calgary but it was the first thing they were going to buy when they got some money together. But she seemed to be a good mother, quite content to look after the baby while her husband slept most of the day away — he was out of the house from 10 P.M. to 8 A.M. every day except Sunday. He'd sold the car the day after they arrived but I'd sometimes see them together in the late afternoon, taking the baby for a walk before dinner. She didn't cook much, or at least very few cooking smells came from the upstairs suite and the delivery boy from the pizzeria showed up a lot at the front door. Danny had certainly kept his word about being quiet — we never heard him go out at night unless we happened to be reading in the sitting-room.

And then one night there was the sound of a TV upstairs, quite loud. I mentioned this to Margie the next day and she turned quite sulky. She was bored at night, she said, with nothing to do and nowhere to go. Danny had borrowed it from one of the fellows at the club. It was company. I explained once again about my exams. She said she'd keep it down. I said no, I didn't want the TV at all and Danny would have to give it back. She gave me a funny smile and shrugged.

"You're the boss."

"That's right," I said, "I am." And tried not to feel guilty at the thought of her upstairs, unable to sleep, unable, even, to go out for a late-night walk because of the sleeping baby. I offered to listen for the baby if she wanted to go out for an hour or so some night.

"Where to?" she said.

"Just for a walk. It's a nice neighbourhood to walk in."

"*Is* it?" she said and smiled that funny smile again.

That night it appeared that Danny hadn't gone to work for we heard the sounds of an argument, low, continuous, furious, long after he usually left the house. The next night there was more argument and then the sound of somebody hammering something to the upstairs door. My husband looked at me as much to say, "It's your problem, you wanted them here," so I went up the stairs and knocked. No answer. I knocked again, louder. Finally a bolt slid back and the door opened a little way. It was held in place by a chain. Margie's face appeared in the crack.

"Oh," she said with a certain relief, "it's you."

"I was wondering about the hammering," I said, "but now I see you were putting on a bolt and chain. You should have asked me before you did that you know. The front door is locked at night; you're perfectly safe."

She just stared at me, a small defiant smile on her face. She said what she had obviously rehearsed.

"We're entitled to some privacy."

"No one is interfering with your privacy in any way," I said. "We've never had a lock on that door because this is an old house and there is no fire escape. However, we would never go up except in an emergency. How would we get to you quickly if the door was locked?"

"There isn't gonna be no emergency," she said, and shut the door in my face.

I went back downstairs and asked my husband what to do.

"Leave it," he said, "we'll remove it when they're gone."

"It's pretty weird," I said. "I think she was expecting someone else to knock on the door, but who? Nobody could get past the front door at night unless they had a key. Do you suppose they've run up some huge debts and are afraid of bill collectors?"

"In two weeks?"

"Maybe in Calgary before they came?"

He smiled. "Just get on with your studying."

I figured they were in some kind of trouble but tried not to think about it — there were only three more weeks until my exams. But the next night, just as I was removing my books and cards from the kitchen table, I heard a noise in the children's room (it was very late, maybe 2 A.M.) and went down the hall to see what it was. A strange man was just shutting the door to the children's room. I was so angry I forgot to be afraid.

"Who are you! What are you doing here!"

"I live here," he said quietly, and went quickly up the stairs to the suite. As I stood at the bottom, my heart pounding, he unlocked the door and went in, drawing the bolt in place as soon as he'd closed the door.

After checking that the children were all right I woke my husband.

"Maybe he's a friend of theirs, just spending the night."

"He said he *lived* here! And the way he said it. Please go and see what's going on, *please*. He was just standing there outside the children's room. I think he'd been in there or was about to go in. I'm *afraid*."

At that my husband put on his dressing-gown and went to investigate. I heard him knock softly, no answer, knock again and again. No one came to the door. He went up again in the morning before work, but there was still no answer.

"Well they can't stay in there forever," he said. "No doubt Margie will come down to do the baby's things and you can ask her what it's all about."

That's when I realized she hadn't been down to do the wash in several days. In fact, I hadn't seen anything of her except for her face at the crack of the upstairs door.

"I think we should call the police," I said.

"Oh come. The man you saw was probably just a friend staying the night who couldn't remember where the stairs were."

"The stairs are right there, as soon as you open the front door!"

"Well maybe he was a bit drunk. Why don't you take a day off and go to the beach with the kids. You've been working too hard."

I resented the implications of that remark but I did go to the beach. I didn't feel like staying in the house alone. I called a friend and she and I and our kids all went for a picnic at Spanish Banks. Afterwards she came back with me and stood at the bottom of the stairs while I went up and knocked, no, pounded, on the upstairs door.

"I really don't like this," I said to my girlfriend. "I'm going to call the police."

"Police, police!" shouted all the kids, very excited. "She's going to call the police!"

At that minute the bolt shot back and Margie, white-faced, anxious, peered out at me.

"Whadya want? You woke the baby up. Why don't you leave us alone?"

"I want to come in for a minute. I want some explanations." I could hear the baby wailing in the other room and the TV turned down low.

"I haven't done nothing," she said, "you're the ones who are always banging on the door."

"I was very frightened to find a strange man in the house last night," I said. "He had a key to the front door and to your door and he said he lives here."

She looked at me, holding her cotton robe together with her free hand, ready to slam the door shut with the other if I should try to force my way in.

"So?" she said.

"So why didn't you tell me you'd invited somebody else to stay with you. You can't do that. We never have more than two people in this suite. I already made an exception for your baby."

"Aren't you wonderful," she said softly, and then, "It's okay, there's only two people here."

"What do you mean? That man said he lived here." (I heard my voice saying "that man.")

"That man's name is Fred and he does live here."

"Where's Danny?"

"Gone," she said, and slammed the door.

"I'm calling the police," I shouted through the door, "right now."

I raced downstairs like a madwoman, shouted, "Don't go!" to my friend and dialled the police. After a bit of explanation I was transferred to the detective in charge of the Boarding House Detail. Sounds like something out of an old radio play, doesn't it, but I assure you it exists, or did in Vancouver in 1963. I can't remember the man's name but he listened patiently for a while and then he broke in to ask me what these people looked like. I described them, sharp-faced Danny, tall, thin Margie and her baby and the Mystery Man. He laughed.

"You sure got yourself mixed up with some lulus," he said, "and there isn't an awful lot I can do about it."

"You *know* these people?"

"I know all of them. Danny and Margie, *not* their real names by the way, are just chicken-shit, if you'll pardon my French —"

"Chicken-shit?"

"Petty thievery, the occasional stolen car, nothing dangerous. I didn't know about the kid. But the other guy — he's not so nice. I wouldn't turn my back on the other guy. If he's who I think he is and he sure sounds like it."

"Can't you come down and arrest them right now?"

"No. There's very little I can do. None of them are wanted for anything — at the minute." He laughed. "They sure sold you a bill of goods."

"I'm scared," I said. "I've got two kids, my husband's away all day and I'm scared."

"Is the third man up there right now?"

"I don't know — I've been at the beach all day.

Margie's up there with the baby, that's all I know.''

He thought a minute. ''Tell her that I want to talk to her.'' And he gave his name.

''She won't come down.''

''I think she will.''

And she did, locking the upstairs behind her, still in the cotton robe. I handed her the phone and went out of the kitchen and into the sitting-room where my girlfriend was trying to keep all the kids amused.

''What's happening?'' she said.

''I'm not sure yet.''

''Are the police coming?'' said the kids.

Margie stuck her head in the sitting-room door. ''He wants to talk to *you*,'' she said. ''It's okay, we're clearing out but we want our money back.'' She gave me such a look of exhausted hate that I've never forgotten it.

I went back into the kitchen and picked up the phone.

''She's going to leave,'' the detective said, ''and the man Fred is out at the minute. You have every legal right to refuse him entry. Go and bolt your front door and just let Margie out or in. According to her, things were getting a bit uncomfortable and Danny's long gone, he won't trouble you. But do me a favour and change your locks just the same. You'll have to give her back the rent.''

''I don't care,'' I said, and then, ''what did you say to her?''

''Never mind. That's between Margie and me.'' He paused. ''I'd like you to do me another favour.''

''What's that.''

''You sound like an intelligent woman and I'm sure you have a warm heart. But the next time you rent to a stranger, even if she looks like your little old grannie, call me and give me a description? What I've done to-day — well, I might not be able to do it again. Fred is not nice, not nice at all.''

I wrote down his name and number, thanked him and

hung up. Margie had gotten dressed and was dragging stuff down the stairs and onto the porch. When everything was out there she went and got the baby and muttered something about going off to the payphone on the corner of Broadway to call a friend. I locked and bolted the door behind her in case Fred came back.

Then I realized she had left the upstairs wide open and I went up, not really out of curiosity but to make sure that she hadn't left anything behind. I couldn't believe what I saw. The TVs, tape recorders, things like that didn't bother me. I'd sort of expected that after talking to the detective. But the floors were filthy, covered in chewing gum, food wrappers, used condoms, spilled pop. The kitchen table had a huge burn where a hot frying pan had been set down on top of it and the whole place stank from a pail of dirty diapers. She had even taken a dirty diaper and rubbed it hard across the kitchen walls.

I stood there, trying to catch my breath. And then I went and stood by the front door, which was glass panelled, and watched her sitting on the porch railing, smoking, the baby in her arms, waiting for her ride. And when her "friend" showed up — it could have been her older sister or her mother, there was a strong family resemblance — I stepped out onto the porch and did something I've always been ashamed of. I shouted at her, as loud as I could, so the whole neighbourhood could hear, "You're trash, that's what you are, just trash!"

Then I went back inside and slammed the door and locked it.

The Happy Farmer

The Happy Farmer

Janet had been reading in bed when she heard a knock on the door. "Come in," she called. Her door was never locked unless she was going to the mainland or Victoria for more than a day.

The knock was repeated. She was recovering from a bad case of flu and had decided to spend the morning in bed. If she stayed quiet whoever it was would go away.

Then she heard the door open and somebody come in.

"Who is it?" she called down. "I've got the flu."

A soft voice, male, replied, "Hi, it's your new neighbour. I came over to say hello."

Janet was surprised that a stranger would walk in when presumably nobody was home. She quickly pulled a sweatshirt over her nightgown and went downstairs. A tall man, his back to her, was examining the photos and cartoons stuck on the fridge.

"Who's that?" he said, without turning around, pointing to a photo on the refrigerator door.

"Let's start with who *you* are. Do you always walk into people's houses when nobody answers the door?"

"I thought maybe you didn't hear me. I could see a light upstairs."

He turned around and smiled at her in a superior way. "Sorry. It *won't* happen again. I came over to introduce myself and borrow a tack hammer, if you've got one. I'm Peter Mahoney and I'll be babysitting the house next door while the Fergusons are in Mexico. I'm an alcoholic." It seemed to her that he said it proudly, as though it were something he'd worked hard to achieve, letters he could put after his name, like MD or CPA. But that was unfair — they had to say it, didn't they, once they'd joined AA? How did one reply? "That's nice" or "How brave of you to admit it" or "Hi, I'm Janet, I'm a divorcée?"

"I don't have a tack hammer," she said. "Use the back of your shoe. I have a regular hammer but that would leave a mark."

"Oh well, it's no big deal." She had a feeling that the tack hammer was just an excuse.

"Do you mind if I sit down?" he said, pulling out a chair.

"Actually, I do." She was surprised to find that she was almost shaking with anger. This guy had some nerve! "I'm just getting over the flu, which is why I didn't answer the door, and I'm spending the day in bed."

"Oh, hey, I didn't mean to get you all upset. Go back to bed and I'll bring you up a cup of tea. Do you have any ginger? Ginger tea is really excellent for flu and colds. Or any garlic? I'd be happy to make you garlic and hot milk."

"And I'd be happy if you'd just leave. I'd really rather be alone. I've just had a cup of tea."

"Ginger tea?" He was turning over the books piled up on the kitchen table. "Heah—vy. Do you really read all this stuff?"

She went to the door and held it open.

"I'd like you to go now. We'll talk some time when I'm better."

Peter got up and bowed his way out of the door, backwards, in a parody of an oriental servant. When he passed her, she could smell the dope. Oh great, she thought, wonderful. She wondered where the Fergusons had found him.

"Bye Janet," he said, and jumped down off the porch. "Hope you get well soon. Hey, what sign are you?"

She shut the door and locked it and went back upstairs. She sensed that he was standing in the yard, grinning. How did he know her name?

The next morning, when she went to get some firewood and let out the hens, she found a small yellow-covered booklet by the front door. *HEAL YOURSELF*, it said, *REVISED EDITION*. Later that day, when her friend Joëlle came over with some soup Janet showed her the book. In the left-hand column of each page was a symptom or disease, in the middle the probable cause and in the right hand, the new thought patterns which would help you get rid of the illness. Joëlle brought up two bowls of soup on a tray and began reading out loud.

" 'Influenza. Response to negativity and beliefs. Fear. Belief in statistics.' And the *cure*, ladies and gentlemen, is to say, 'I am beyond group beliefs or the calendar. I am free from all congestion and influence.' How can you say all that if you are coughing your little lungs out?"

"You can think it, I guess," Janet said. "You don't need to say it out loud."

" 'Ingrown toenail'," Joëlle read, " 'Insanity, Insomnia, Itching.' What a load of *marde*."

"It would be funny, except people probably believe it and then feel worse when the insanity doesn't go away."

"If you are insane," Joëlle said, "if you are *fou*, how

are you going to understand enough to say the mantras or whatever this stuff is called?''

"Good point. But read out the one on AIDS. I'll bet you didn't know you could cure AIDS through the power of positive thinking.''

" 'AIDS. Denial of the self. Sexual guilt. A strong belief in not being good enough.' And you say, 'I am a Divine, magnificent expression of life. I rejoice in my sexuality. I love myself.' ''

"I looked at alcoholism, of course," Janet said, "because he said he was an alcoholic.''

" 'Live in the now. I choose to see my self-worth' blah blah blah. Well, maybe it worked for him." She handed back the book.

"That's true. I'm probably being unfair to both him *and* the book. It worked for him and now he feels he has to proselytize. But there's something creepy about him, something menacing. The way he walked right in. I got the feeling that he would have come in and examined everything whether I'd been home or not. And he's got one of those soft voices, you know the kind. You just know he never raises his voice and is full of anger.''

"Those sixties voices. Peace and Love. We all tried to talk like that in the sixties." Joëlle softened her voice, turned it right down to simmer. "Oh, I feel so at one with Nature over here. I think I'll just lie down and *foquer* this tree." She grinned. "We were like that in Quebec you know; you guys on the West Coast didn't have a monopoly on that stuff.''

"He smokes dope, as well.''

"Well, voila! A throwback to the Golden Age. He's not the only one on this island.''

"Would AA allow him to smoke dope?''

Joëlle shrugged. "I don't know. Shall we ring up and ask them?''

"You think I'm being silly.''

"I think you are being just a teeney-tiny bit paranoid."

"I know I am. I locked my door after he left. And then today I remembered that the Fergusons have an emergency set of keys to this place and they are so organized no doubt the keys are hanging by the back door labelled 'Janet'."

"Listen, *ma pitoune*, if he tries to get smart with you just give us a call and Bernard and me will jump into our clothes and come down and beat him up, okay?"

"Okay."

But it bothered her — he bothered her. Although he didn't actually knock on her door for the next two weeks, he left her little gifts on the doorstep — a knob of ginger-root; a weird drawing of a man and a woman falling through space, reaching out their arms to one another; a bottle of Blue Nun; another book, by somebody who had taken the name of Shastri. She never heard him come up on the porch and wondered if he waited until all her lights were off and she was safely asleep.

One morning she found him leaning over the fence, talking to her hens. He was holding a violin.

"Hi there," he said. "Want me to feed them for you? I really get off on that old rooster of yours."

She wondered if he was being sarcastic. The rooster had just graduated to rooster status and he crowed whenever the spirit moved him, which was often. Janet had nicknamed him "Don," for Don Giovanni and a Mafia don. He had the hens right where he wanted them.

"I hope his crowing doesn't disturb you," she said. "This bird has given new meaning to the word 'dawn'."

"Oh nothing disturbs *me*," he said, pointing his bow at her in a mocking manner. "I hope my playing doesn't disturb *you*. I decided to learn the violin while I'm out here on vacation."

Vacation from *what*? she wondered, but she didn't ask, just shook her head again and emptied the compost bucket and the pan of laying pellets into the chicken run. She wanted to tell him to stay off her land but couldn't think of any valid reason for doing so.

"Are you finished with those books I lent you?" he said. "What did you think?"

"I haven't had time to look at them. I'll get them right now."

"No no, that's cool. I just wondered if you'd had a chance to peek at them. Those books changed my life." He was talking to her back, following a few steps behind her as she made for the house. She wanted to run and then slam the door in his face, push the bureau against it, phone Joëlle and Bernard. But why? He hadn't done anything except be a little forward, a little pushy. It was just a difference of personalities.

He followed her in, stopping to take his gumboots off as she did, before stepping onto the kitchen floor.

"I don't suppose you have time for a cup of tea?" he said.

"No I don't." She went quickly up the stairs to get the books. When she came back he was again peering at the photos and cartoons on her fridge.

"Who's the guy? Your husband?" He was sure he knew all about her by now. He had taken to sitting down below on the porch of the general store, with some of the other men who supported themselves and their women (and sometimes children) doing odd jobs of all kinds.

"A friend," she said, non-committal, and held out the books as well as the wine and the joints.

"Do you sleep with him?"

"Here you are," she said. "Thanks for the offer of all this, but I can't use any of it."

He gave her a wide-eyed, innocent smile. "Not use the *wine*? Hey, are you AA too?"

"No." Joëlle said the girls were crazy about him, thought he was the handsomest unattached male who had come to the island in a long time. Janet supposed he was handsome, in a gangly, boyish kind of way. He was somewhere between thirty and forty, hard to tell. His alcoholism certainly hadn't affected his looks.

"I have to get to work now," she said.

"Janet, Janet." He shook his head. His hair was pepper and salt and came well down below his ears. Whatever he had being doing before he came here, it had allowed him to grow his hair. "You don't like me, do you? You don't give a fellow a chance." He made no attempt to take the things she was holding out to him.

"Two lonely people," he mourned.

"I'm not lonely," she said.

"No of course not. Okay, one lonely person then, your neighbour, and you reject him out of hand."

"I want you to go now," she said. What she really wanted to do was take the bottle of Blue Nun and smash it over his head.

"I'm goin', I'm goin'," he said. He balanced the things on top of his violin. "Some other time."

The next time she went to the store he was sitting on the porch eating a veggieburger. He said something very low to the fellows sitting near him and they laughed. Most of these guys had worked for her at one time or another and she'd thought they all liked and respected her. Their laughter hurt. She remembered a new girl at school, years ago, who had taken her best friend away from her. She had the same sort of powerless feeling now. The new girl had had a horse named Stormy Rex. What did Peter have? Well, he was male, to begin with, and no doubt he had good dope.

"What do you care what those jerks say?" Joëlle frowned. "It's not like you to get upset about gossip."

"I know. I don't understand it myself. He's not even a permanent fixture — somebody I'd really have to accept as a neighbour. He'll be gone in a month or so. I just think he's playing some kind of game and it makes me nervous."

"You want me to lend you Samson?" Samson was Joëlle's German Shepherd/Husky cross. She had got him when she was living alone in the city, before she met Bernard. "He will bite the nuts off any guy who bothers you."

"No, that's okay. But thanks."

"This guy, I think he is, in reality, harmless. Just another ass to warm the bench outside the store."

"I wish he'd stop leaving me little 'presents'."

"I'll get Samson to leave him *un p'tit cadeau*, a big shit right on his doorstep."

But it was Peter who got a dog, a black Lab he called Fang. He also acquired an old Dodge pick-up and drove up and down the island in his truck, with Fang sitting in the back, his pink tongue hanging out. Janet and Joëlle had a theory that some enterprising person could make a lot of money creating artificial dogs out of something like papier mâché, only waterproof. They could even have batteries inside so their heads would turn and their mouths open. They could be bolted in the backs of station wagons and pick-up trucks and would save people the trouble of having a live dog, while still allowing them to look like real islanders. Peter and another fellow were now in the business of cutting and selling firewood. He offered Janet a cut-rate price. Fang was watching the hens, fascinated, his nose up against the chicken wire. He was going to get pecked if he didn't watch out.

"No thanks."

"Looks to me like you're runnin' low on wood. Or is your friend comin' to cut you some?"

"My friend?"

"The fellow on the fridge. Is he away or somethin'?" Peter had taken to dropping the g's off the end of his words so that he would sound more "country." One night he had stood under her window and played his violin, the same tune over and over, "The Happy

Farmer.'' Janet recognized it from her childhood music lessons.

Joëlle and some of the other women were getting pissed off because he was very liberal with the dope.

''At least you don't have to live next door to him. And speaking of dope, he left me a big bucket of compost yesterday, with a note 'for Don Giovanni and the Ladies.' I got suspicious and went through it. He had loaded it with dope.''

Joëlle laughed. ''The hens would have had a good time!''

''Maybe. Or they might have gone nuts. Remember when everybody who went tree-planting also dropped a little marijuana here and there? There were an awful lot of stoned birds flying around, bumping into things and killing themselves. He knows I sell some of the eggs; maybe he wanted to see if people would get high from the eggs. It's all so childish and stupid.''

''Did you tell him?''

''He knows what I think of him.''

He sat on the porch of the store with his buddies. When Janet went in he said to Fang, patting his head, ''The lady next door don't like me, nope, she don't like me at *all*.''

''Hey Janet,'' he called one day, ''have you ever been to Greece?''

She shook her head and he got up and followed her into the store. ''Well I was in Crete in the seventies, in Matala, and you know what they call hens in Greece? Do you?'' He was dancing around her as she picked out milk from the cooler, a couple of tomatoes.

''They call a hen *'kotopoulo,'* stupid bird. Isn't that cute? Some of the Greek men say that about women too, especially North American women who go down there and parade around in bikinis or short shorts that cut right up into their crotch. *Kotopoulo!*''

The storekeeper was grinning as he rang up her groceries.

"Fuck off, Peter," she said, when he wouldn't let her get out the door.

"Now that's not *nice*. That's not *neighbourly*. I'll let you go but first I want to tell you about a strange dream I had last night. I nearly came over and woke you up it distressed me so. I —"

"Tell him to get away from the door," Janet said to the storekeeper.

"Let her go, Peter."

Peter shrugged and opened the door for her with an elaborate bow.

"I dreamt I was havin' sex with my mother," he said, following her to the bottom of her path, speaking very loud so the men on the porch could hear. "But not just ordinary sex — she was suckin' me off. You're an educated woman, what do you suppose that means? My *mother* suckin' me off. I must be in a bad way, hey? Desperate for it. Soon I'll be humping table-legs, like old Fang here."

He stayed at the bottom but his voice followed her up the path. She was so angry she was shaking. She wanted to call the police, but what could she charge him with? She had a feeling they would just laugh at her. Had he actually threatened her in any way? "No, not really, not physically. It's a kind of mental harassment." She could imagine the sergeant or whatever he was, on the other end of the line, in Ganges. "I see." He would give her a kindly lecture about neighbours in the country having to get along with one another, how her real neighbours, what was their name again, would be back soon and this guy would be gone. However, if he actually *threatened* her she was, of course, to call back immediately. He would suggest she get a dog.

Janet had inherited her hens from her friend Louise, who moved into the city when her son was old enough to go to high school. She knew she'd never be able to keep them in the city. At the time there had been five hens and five chicks, one of whom had grown into the handsome rooster with his black-green tail feathers and his exuberant crow. Janet hired a fellow to make a chicken house next to the vegetable garden and Louise donated chicken wire for the run. It was risky to let them range freely as the raccoons were numerous and greedy. Tourists thought raccoons were cute, and fed them. There were mink also. Hens were high on the list of preferred foods for both raccoons and mink. Even with a fenced-in run, she was always careful to shut them in their house by nightfall. She didn't really know much about hens and now that she was living alone she certainly didn't want all the eggs, but she easily found buyers for the surplus and Louise advised her on laying pellets and hen scratch. Janet also gave them all her kitchen compost plus old produce from the store. She didn't exactly *like* them, the way one might like — or even love — a cat or dog, but she grew fond of them and even, on cold days, cooked them up mashed potatoes and gave them hot milk with their mash. They rewarded her with a lot of eggs and she was keeping the money in a jar until she had enough to buy some splendid piece of lawn furniture. Two of the hens were exotic and laid eggs with pale green shells. When friends came on weekends Janet always made sure they went away with a few green eggs. And she never had any trouble finding people to let them out, feed them, put them back in again if she wanted to go away. Joëlle usually did it, or the Fergusons, or the young couple at the store. Whoever did this got to keep the eggs. She wouldn't have *chosen* to have hens — she was trying to keep herself free of all encumbrances — but now that they were here she rather liked the idea.

"How dare I laugh at all these people in overalls, with pick-up trucks and dogs," she said to Joëlle, "when I have a mason jar labelled 'egg money.' "

One morning Janet found a letter on her doorstep. She recognized Peter's handwriting. He hadn't bothered her for over a week and her first thought was to throw it in the fire, but curiosity got the better of her. The note was printed, and was quite long; it was about her hens.

"Janet," it began. "I once worked on a farm in Ontario, which included care of three hundred chickens. I learned a lot about fowl care at the time, forgotten most of it, but seeing your hens every day, and the conditions <u>they are forced to endure</u> has brought back some memories I had displaced somewhere in the recesses of my feeble mind. Would it offend you if I took it upon myself to make some suggestions at this point? Being a 'lover' (of animals of <u>all</u> <u>types</u>!!) I even have feelings for chickens, who are not really as stupid as the Greeks and others among us think (but that is a whole 'nother story)."

He then proceeded to tell her all the things she was doing wrong. The birds were grossly underweight, the nesting boxes should be cleaned twice, not once, a week "at least" (underlined), the rooster could get fungus under his feet. The chicken run was too small — they should be allowed to range freely. The raccoons would not attack in the daytime.

"I gave them, yesterday, when you were at the South End, a bag of natural birdseed (barley, sunflower, wheat, etc.) and they went crazy for it, so it seems they were hungry.

"Lots of fun doing the 'farm bit' but you have to take it <u>seriously</u>.

Peace,
Your friend Peter."

Janet went out and looked at the hens and the rooster. They looked fat and healthy, but what did she know about it? Louise had told her what they needed and she had simply followed instructions. They laid well and they weren't fighting with one another. Their combs were bright red and she seemed to recall, from something she'd read, that that was a sign of healthy chickens. She knew that if the letter had come from anyone else she would have been much more receptive, but she didn't want to enter into a conversation with Peter, for whatever reason, and she was afraid to let the hens run free. Other people on the island had whole flocks wiped out in one day. Maybe when spring came and the days were longer, she would try them two at a time, so she wouldn't be chasing all ten back into the chicken house at once. If those two didn't wander very far, then she could advance to four, six, eight, and so on. There were the dogs to think about as well. Would the various dogs leave her chickens alone?

She sealed the letter back up and left it under the mat.

A few days later she had to go to Vancouver for two days. Joëlle and Bernard had left for Mexico to get some sun and her neighbours on the other side from the Fergusons were away in Hawaii. She asked the couple at the store to chicken-sit, in return for the eggs, and they said they wouldn't mind at all. They were already minding Samson, who never worried the hens.

When she came back the yard was full of feathers and bits of chickens and the door to the chicken house was wide open.

Peter must have heard her drive up. He was in the yard almost as soon as she was.

"Hi," he said. "I was hoping to get this cleaned up before you got back. It's a real shame."

Janet could hardly speak. She ran down the path and banged on the door of the store. It was a Monday, and they were closed. She banged and banged until they had to come see what was the matter.

"What happened to my chickens! You said you'd take care of them."

The storekeeper looked surprised. "What's the problem?"

"The *problem* is that they are all dead. Killed. By raccoons or mink or dogs or *something*. They are all in little pieces in my yard. I *stepped* on the rooster's head!" She began to cry.

"Listen, Janet, I don't know anything about this."

"Did you forget, was that it? You just forgot?"

"No I didn't forget. Peter offered to do it for me, since we were really busy over the weekend. He just lived next door — it was easier for him. I'm awfully sorry, but he offered, and well —" He held out his hands, palms up, and shrugged.

Peter was picking up chicken bits and feathers and putting them in a garbage bag. Fang was going crazy, worrying pieces of feather and flesh.

"You let them out, didn't you? You let them out and left them out."

Peter looked up from his job. "Honestly, Janet, I just meant to let them out for a few hours. They were desperate to be free. You've never been in prison, I have. They were desperate to be out of there. I was just goin' to give them a little parole, a kind of day pass, and then, with one thing and another —"

"You got stoned and forgot about them. You left them out all night."

He smiled sadly. "I remembered when I heard all the noise. Fang and I came rushin' over but it was too late. There were about six or seven coons. Those coons are vicious — they really hissed at us, man. I thought they were goin' to go for Fang." He paused. "We chased them off but the chickens were already dead."

"Get off my land," Janet said. "Get off and don't ever come on it again. I think you did this on purpose. I think you deliberately 'forgot' about them once you let them out and I think you deliberately left this mess until I got back."

"That's not a very nice accusation," he said.

"I don't think you're a very nice person."

"Those hens weren't happy, Janet. They were desperate for their freedom. I know they're dead now and that's awful, that's tragic, but they did enjoy a few hours of freedom. Maybe it was their Karma to die.''

"Get out — just go.''

Janet began stuffing chicken bits into the garbage bag. There seemed to be hundreds of them. It was as though the chickens had been hacked to bits rather than mauled by raccoons. The raccoons left mostly heads and feet. She hadn't realized they were such fussy eaters.

She stopped. Dumped out what she had just picked up. Dumped out what Peter had been picking up. Then she carefully tidied up the entire mess, put it in the garbage bag and fastened it with a twist-tie and drove to the community dump and then back home, making one or two stops along the way.

It was nearly dark by the time she began on the chicken house. First the door had to come off its hinges, then the window prised out, then the pen cut away with wire-cutters. Janet didn't like to use a chain-saw but she knew how and figured it was the best and quickest way to get the structure down.

The roof she just smashed in with a crowbar, and as she wrecked the chicken house she hummed ''The Happy Farmer.''

She was nearly finished when Peter came rushing over from next door. She had known it would take quite a while for him to connect her with the chain-saw and the banging. The Fergusons' sitting-room was at the front of their house and no doubt he had been watching TV. TV was acceptable if you were selective, he said.

''Hey Janet! What are you doin', man?''

Janet put down the saw and smiled at him.

''I was going to come over and knock on your door just as soon as I washed up.''

''But what have you done?''

She began to stack the pieces of wood, ready for sawing up in the morning.

''I realize I owe you a debt of gratitude, Peter, and I wanted to come over and tell you so.''

''What're you talkin' about? I let your chickens die.''

"That's just it. When I went inside to get another bag I realized I felt some sadness, sure, but also a great relief. I'm sorry for the way they died but I'm glad to be rid of them. Really. Too much hassle. I guess it really was their Karma that you forgot to put them in. Or my Karma, maybe.''

"But Janet —''

She walked towards her house. "What you said about 'desperate for freedom,' well — that really hit me where it hurt. They were probably destroyed anyway — emotionally I mean. There's more to life than being a good layer.''

"But Janet!'' He hurried after her.

"It's okay. I feel wonderful, actually. I feel — well, I guess I feel liberated. I'm going to make a little memorial omelette just now and light a candle, then have a good long soak and go to bed. Good-night, Peter.'' She was up on the porch now, nearly to the door. She'd have to go back for the tools after he left.

He caught her sleeve. "But Janet, I didn't let the chickens die — it was all a joke.''

"That's all right, Peter. You don't have to pretend.''

"I swear to you, Janet, it was a joke. I just wanted to break through that wall you keep around yourself — see you really express yourself emotionally. The chickens are safe. I got Fred to pick up a bag of chicken stuff at the poultry farm in Sidney. He's got the chickens — and the rooster — down at his place.''

She turned and faced him under the front porch light. What a silly-looking guy he was. Janet wondered what he had really been before he decided to be an ex-con and an aging hippie. A used-car salesman perhaps. What was the matter with her that she'd been so afraid of him? She laughed out loud. She laughed right in his stupid face.

"If that's really true, Peter, then you're going to be very busy for the next little while, building me a new hen house. At your expense. What a pity I smashed everything up so badly. You'd better get started first thing in the morning as I'd like the hens back by tomorrow night and nicely settled. Otherwise the cops. You might see the inside of a jail cell yet."

She went in and shut the door behind her.

"It was all a joke!" he cried from the other side.

Janet opened the door again.

"And I'm laughing," she said, *"bonsoir."*

The Survival
of
the Fittest

The Survival
of
the Fittest

Whenever her daughter or son-in-law said "fibre optics," Mrs Hutchison had a mental image of bolts of cloth printed with enormous eyes. Her late father had been sales manager for a Manchester textile factory and this particular factory printed yards and yards of fabric destined for West African markets. It used to be called "Mammy cloth," because it was the "mammies," or market women, who sold it, although one probably couldn't say that now. From time to time her father would bring home a yard or two of one of the more flamboyant designs — green crocodiles on a mustard yellow background, for example, or the heads of political leaders or football stars, once a young woman in a mini-skirt, dancing against an Easter-purple background with a slogan printed underneath: MINI MINI MINI LOOK AT ME.

"Fancy walking around the town with Winston Churchill on your backside," he said. For the women went to the markets and bought this stuff and made it up into skirts and dresses, or, in the villages, just wrapped it around themselves. Men too — they had it made into shirts or bought twelve yards and wore it as a kind of toga, wrapped and folded and one end flung over their shoulder. Her father had made two trips to what was then the Gold Coast and brought back pictures to show them.

"Against their skin," he said to his wife and daughter, "and in that setting, it really looks quite nice." Some of the women in the photographs had bare breasts, with torpedo-shaped nipples. She found it embarrassing to think of her father taking such photos, and it must have bothered her mother as well, for after a few days the pictures disappeared. Perhaps he gave them to the owners of the factory.

She knew fibre optics had nothing to do with any of this, but because she didn't understand one bit of the explanation her daughter and son-in-law gave her, except that it allowed messages to zoom around the globe at unimaginable speeds, the image of the Mammy cloth persisted. And now, because she was so feverish, every time she closed her own eyes against the headache that was getting worse and worse in spite of the paracetamol she had taken just before boarding the train, all she saw were variations on the cloth printed with eyes. Sometimes the eyes were brown, wide open against green palm branches and a blue sky; sometimes the eyes themselves were bright blue and set into the tail feathers of yellow birds; sometimes they simply grew on red stalks and were every colour of the rainbow.

"Are you sure you're all right, Mum? Are you positive you don't want me to go with you as far as Boulogne? I'm worried about you travelling alone." Heather had married an American and her accent, although still Glasgow, had an overlay of American. She arranged her mother's bag and bits and pieces on the rack above her head and now sat facing her, frowning. This was one of the old-fashioned trains with compartments, plush seats and windows that opened.

"You're *sure*?"

Mrs Hutchison wasn't at all sure but she bravely nodded her head. She felt terribly ill and light-headed, but Heather was only six weeks out of hospital with her baby, now waiting at home with the woman in the next flat. Heather was breast-feeding; how could she go all the way to Boulogne and back? Impossible.

"I'm sure."

"Well you can't go wrong. Just get off at the last stop and follow the crowd. I'm glad you've got that little wheelie thing as I don't know if there are any porters at the Hovercraft — I've never taken it. But this is the fastest way to cross. Joe says it's boring, but fast. He calls it the longest car wash in the world."

Mrs Hutchison had never been on a Hovercraft either, and she was apprehensive. To her, a young girl during the war, the word "hover" reminded her too much of the V-1 rockets that cut out before they fell. She and her mother used to wait in the awful silence and darkness, holding hands and counting. *"Aeroglisseur,"* it said on her ticket. She didn't like speed: if she hadn't felt so poorly she would have gone back the way she came, by ship. She had crossed over from Dover and enjoyed that very much. Joe and Heather were completely reliable — she knew they would be waiting at the barrier at the Gare du Nord, looking out for her and smiling. She hadn't minded any of it — the long trip down from Edinburgh and then the boat train to Dover, the ferry and the train to Paris. It was an adventure and she had left home well fortified with sandwiches, two thermoses of tea and a good novel. Now it seemed to her impossible that she would be able to make all these connections, the Hovercraft, the boat-train to Charing Cross. She'd have to take a taxi to King's Cross — she would be too ill to manage the tube.

It was a weekday and the second train from Paris to Boulogne. After Heather left she was alone in the compartment. Every so often she heard singing and shouting

along the corridor — the football rowdies. She and
Heather had seen them at the station.

She was glad Joe wasn't like that. When Heather had
written from America that she had fallen in love with a
man from Connecticut (Mrs Hutchison pronounced it
"con-neckt-ee-cut") she uttered a little cry of dismay.
And was immediately ashamed of herself. The gum-
chewing, loud-talking man in an Hawaiian shirt — the
man conjured up by the word "American" — was just as
ridiculous as the kilt-wearing, haggis-eating, pinch-penny
Scot that the Americans thought of whenever a Scotsman
was mentioned. Or her Uncle Alf' saying about the
French — "Wogs begin at Calais."

Joe turned out to be a tall, thin, shy man whose French
co-workers called him the asparagus. His sandy hair was
receding a bit at the temples and he had a big smile — the
smile the only truly "American" thing about him
perhaps — and lovely teeth. It was obvious that he loved
her daughter very much — the way he touched the back
of her hand when talking to someone else, the way he said
her name. Mrs Hutchison had loved her own husband in
a quiet, contented sort of way but he was not a very affectionate man. Watching Heather and Joe and the baby she
realized she had missed out on that — the little everyday
gestures of affection. And yesterday, when Joe had walked
into the flat with one of those long French loaves, he had
stuck it in front of him, down by his crotch, when he
thought his mother-in-law wasn't looking. Heather began
to laugh. It wasn't nasty, the way Joe did it, and you
could feel the affection between them, the passion even.
Sandy Hutchison had been a passionate man — passionate about politics, about labour unions, about her
body even — but he had not been affectionate or playful.
On rainy days, when Heather was small, she would poke
her finger into his newspaper and demand, "What I can
do, Daddy?" and he would lower the newspaper and look

at her in distress. If she'd been a boy it might have been different.

Nevertheless, he had been a good man and a good provider and she wished with all her heart that he were here beside her and not dead these last three years. He was absolutely dependable, except when he did the strange thing of keeling over with a massive heart attack in Queen Street Station. He died on the way to hospital — they never even had a chance to say goodbye. He never met Joe. Heather's letter arrived three days after the funeral. On the telephone she had offered to come home for a few weeks but her mother said no. The neighbours were very kind and there wasn't really anything that she could do.

"Just be with you?" Heather suggested.

Her mother tried to imagine Heather standing in her flat — her "apartment" — in Boston, talking into a telephone, maybe a fancy one like one of those she saw advertised the week before when she went to pay her telephone bill. There were pictures of all sorts of telephones, for executives and people in a hurry, telephones with memories, telephones without cords, Princess phones in pretty colours, even telephones for the kiddies — shaped like Snoopy or Mickey Mouse. One advertisement had amused her in a grim way, an ad for a "grannie phone." There was a picture of a sweet-looking, white-haired lady, face down on the carpet, and underneath the words — "Thirty seconds after she fell, help was on the way." It seemed you just yelled "help help" and the telephone picked up the sound of your voice. It was the same as dialling 999. When her turn came at the counter she said to the girl, "Grandpas fall down as well," and pointed to the ad. The girl was busy; she didn't even smile.

"I don't know, I'm sure," she said, handing back the change and dismissing her. "Next," she called, as Mrs Hutchison moved away.

Just before they hung up, Heather asked shyly,

"Mum, did you get my December thirtieth letter?"

"Not yet — was there something special? Is anything wrong?"

"I'll call you next week. You should have read it by then. It's something nice."

That was the letter about Joe, a man she'd met months ago at a concert. They were going to get married, quietly — his parents were dead. They would both be coming over together in the summer.

And now they were living in Paris for two years and had named their daughter Margaret, after her. Joe was forty and Heather thirty-seven; this might be the only child.

The headache was terrible now, sickening. How did she say in French, "Help me, I am ill?" How would she get through this day? She took two more tablets although it wasn't four hours since the last, washing them down with some bottled water Heather had bought for her. "Fancy paying for water!" her mother said the first time they went out to a restaurant. "It seems a wicked waste of money."

"My mother's become a true Scot," Heather said, and they all laughed.

Mrs Hutchison fell asleep. When she awoke the countryside was shrouded in fog. At first she thought she was so ill she couldn't see properly but no, the fog was real, rolling in across the fields and farmhouses. They must be getting near the coast. She stood on the seat to take down her things. The headache was still there but distant, like a growling dog behind a gate. She moved as carefully as she could, given the rocking of the train — she didn't want to aggravate the headache in any way.

The men who had come over for some football match or other were shouting and singing in the corridor directly outside her compartment — belching loudly, and showing off.

> Ou ay leh pap-pee-yay
> Ou ay leh pap-pee-yay . . .

They had the thick phlegmy voices of the Midlands, Birmingham perhaps. People like these gave Britain a bad name. Heather said all the trouble with the football fans could be laid at the feet of Thatcher and unemployment but Mrs Hutchison wasn't so sure. She thought that was just an excuse, like the people who got drunk at parties or in pubs and said mean, nasty things they didn't remember the next day. They were mean, nasty people to begin with. And men in groups often behaved like idiots, egging one another on. Schoolboys.

The train slowed down and stopped with a series of jerks. She did as Heather had told her and followed the crowd to the Hoverport. The fog was very thick and she kept her woollen scarf wrapped tightly around her neck. Nearly everyone headed for the Duty Free before they went to the sign that said *CONTROLES*, but Mrs Hutchison just wanted to sit down somewhere until the flight, if that's what you called it, was announced.

An elderly couple moved over on a bench when they saw her looking around. They had two large carrier bags that clunked and clanked when they shifted them. They were from Dover, they said, and had come over to France just for the day. They came regularly just to buy wine and tobacco. "We don't touch spirits," the wife said.

"But now it looks as though we may be stuck here," she said.

"Stuck here?"

"The fog," said the husband. "These Hovercraft are all very well but they can't operate in the fog, you know — too dangerous."

Mrs Hutchison wanted to weep. She willed her husband back from the grave, Heather and Joe down from Paris, somebody known and beloved to lean on. She didn't think she could bear a delay.

"They've been announcing it in English as well as French," said the woman. " 'Adverse weather conditions.' You listen — you'll hear the announcement in a few minutes."

When Heather was a small girl her godmother gave her a doll with a china head. Mrs Hutchison decided to put it away until the child was old enough to take care of it properly. It was far too fine a gift for a child of three. The doll had real hair, tiny white teeth and clear blue eyes that opened and shut. She wrapped the doll in tissue paper and put it in the bottom drawer of the wardrobe. But a few months later Heather managed to get the drawer open. She banged the doll's head on the bathroom floor until the smiling face was all in pieces. She told her mother, who discovered her weeping loudly (in fear, not sorrow), that she had wanted to see how the eyes worked. They turned out to be attached to rubber bands. The man from Dover had eyes the same colour as that doll, and Mrs Hutchison was sorry she had thought of it, for now, when she shut her eyes against the re-emerging pain of her headache and the noise of all the people talking and shouting, she saw dozens and dozens of blue glass eyes held together with rubber bands. And she saw her own face cracked in several places. This was worse than the Mammy cloth; this was somehow sinister, frightening. She was a practical woman and not much given to fancies, but she was becoming more and more uneasy. Perhaps she shouldn't cross tonight, in this fog. There must be an information booth somewhere. She would take a room in the town and have a good sleep. Her illness would be gone in the morning. She couldn't help thinking of the *Herald of Free Enterprise*. Joe and Heather wouldn't laugh at her if she telephoned and said she'd decided not to cross tonight.

"Sheep," said a Frenchwoman's crackling voice over the loudspeaker, "we apologize for the sheep's delay."

"You've not bought anything from the Duty Free?" said the wife from Dover, rather accusingly.

"No," Mrs Hutchison replied, "no." She tried to smile. "Actually, what I'd rather like just now is a nice cup of tea."

"Oh, you won't get a nice cup of tea over on *this* side,"

said the husband. "The French aren't much on *tea*." The
rubber bands moved his eyes from side to side. "You're a
fool, however, if you don't mind my saying so, not to take
advantage of the low price on drink. No offence."

"I suppose I am," Mrs Hutchison said. What did they
do with all those bottles? They didn't have the faces of
heavy drinkers. She had a feeling that it was the idea of a
bargain they liked. She imagined a bungalow or a semi-
detached with rooms full of unopened bottles.

"I've been to Paris to see my daughter," Mrs Hutchison offered. "She's married to an American and they've
been transferred to Paris for two years."

"We met a lot of Americans during the war," the old
man said.

"Oh yes *indeed*," said his wife in a sarcastic tone.

"Went to an American mess once," her husband said.
"They ate their sweet along with their meat. Extraordinary people." He did not seem to think that he and his
wife were at all extraordinary, beetling back and forth
across the Channel and never seeing anything but the Duty Free Shops.

But now something was happening, the French
woman's voice was giving out new information. Those
who could understand the French were already up and
heading for the exits when she spoke again in English.
Due to the weather the Hovercraft would not be crossing
the Channel. There were buses outside to take them to
the ferry terminal. They would have to take a ship to
Dover. A train would be waiting. More apologies.

When Mrs Hutchison stood up she thought she was going to fall over. And the noise! The departure hall was
made of concrete; sound bounced off the walls, shouts, a
babble of French and English. She was drowning in a
gigantic swimming bath. Hundreds of bottles clanked in
their plastic bags. It was as though they were all prisoners
wearing some strange kind of manacles made of water-
filled glass.

An argument broke out when a woman was jostled by

one of the football fans and her bag dropped to the floor.
"Here, Missus," he shouted, "Yer drinks leakin'!" He
was wearing a pair of women's tights on his head.

"Scum," the woman screamed at him, "you're
nothing but scum."

"Piss off," said the drunken fan.

The crowd paid no attention, just surged around them
as though they were two rocks in a stream.

"If I can get outside," thought Mrs Hutchison, "if I
can get outside into the air maybe I can breathe." She
had seen a fire-eater once at a county fair. Her lungs felt
scorched, as though she too had swallowed fire, as though
the fog which had seeped into the building was really
smoke and deadly gases. What had Sandy thought, in the
middle of the crowd at Queen Street Station, unable to
catch his breath?

Outside it was worse. The fog was so thick they could
hear the water but they couldn't see it. And there was a
wind blowing sharp sand. Nobody queued, but pushed
and shoved their way onto the buses. The Hovercraft
stewardesses, holding tight to their ridiculous Princess
Anne hats, called out that there was plenty of room, plenty of room for all of you, please step to the rear of the bus.

Mrs Hutchison stood on the overloaded bus, her face
pressed into the back of a rough tweed jacket smelling of
cigarettes and dog. She kept her mind firmly fixed on her
cosy flat back in Edinburgh. As soon as she got home she
would fill a hot-water bottle and make herself a pot of tea.
When Sandy came in from union meetings, shivering and
hoarse, he used to pour a tot of whisky in his tea. Perhaps
she would do that. And sleep. Sleep until she woke. Mrs
Philpot, across the stair, was to turn on the immersion
heater and light the fire in the lounge. It might be a good
idea to ring her from Dover. And Heather and Joe as
well, just so they wouldn't worry.

The football fans were singing rude songs again.

"— line them up against the wall and shoot them,

that's what I'd like to do,'' came a disapproving voice from behind her left ear. ''Dis-gus-ting.''

Last Saturday, on the late train back from Glasgow, where she'd gone to visit an elderly cousin of her husband, there had been a policewoman, a policeman and a dog. All the football fans were herded into the last two coaches. The world seemed to be full of angry men. She was glad Heather was with a gentle man like Joe. When men were angry they attacked whatever was weakest and nearest.

Joe said, quite simply, ''I love her; I can no longer imagine my life without her.'' And now, here was the baby — Margaret. She hadn't said so, but she was glad the baby was a girl. It was hard for a boy to grow up gentle, however much his parents might wish it so.

Another wait, more apologies in French and English — the sheep the sheep the sheep. Mrs Hutchison was covered in a clammy sweat and she had begun to cough. It was nearly 5 P.M. She should have been an hour away from London by now, on the train, and she was still in France.

''Why are we wait-ting / Oh why are we wait-ting'' sang the football rowdies.

Now, when she shut her eyes she saw nothing but flashes of colour. ''I am really terribly ill,'' she thought, and then, ''I don't want to die in France.'' Her father had been at Dieppe. How many times had he shut his eyes and prayed, ''I don't want to die in France.'' She tried to concentrate on her tea-kettle, her hand holding a hot-water bottle, her cosy bed with the downie Heather and Joe had given her for her birthday last year. She had been reluctant to use it at first, having been brought up with the idea that for a good night's sleep you needed to be weighed down with several layers of British wool. Now she loved it.

The ship came, finally, and the great crowd (for not only were there two loads of Hovercraft patrons by now but also all those who had tickets for the ferry) surged on board. No question of women and children first, no question of courtesy or queuing. All tables and chairs were quickly snatched up. Twice Mrs Hutchison attempted to sit on an empty chair only to be told that the seats were being saved.

"I'm not very well," she said, "I need to sit down."

"These seats are taken."

She sat on the floor, in a corner, afraid even to go to the loo although her bladder was bursting. Above her head she heard a man say that the ferry was dreadfully overloaded and he was going to write a letter to the company as soon as he got home. Another voice said somebody had been sick in the gents. She was burning up.

Standing by the carousel, waiting for her luggage, reduced by her pain and fever to a character in her own dream, Mrs Hutchison heard some familiar Manchester accents. Two couples, smartly dressed, laughing and joking with one another. She gathered up her courage and went over to speak to them, to ask if by any chance they were taking the train from London. She did not care that she must have looked a sight, grimy, with flyaway hair and her face as red as a lobster.

Brenda and Phil, David and Dorothy. They watched her bags while she went to the Ladies; they helped her find the telephones; they found her a place on the boat-train and hovered over her protectively. Phil told her how he had met some public-school boys on the ferry who said they wished the trespassing laws were more strict so that trespassers could be shot. He shook his head. When the football rowdies lurched into their coach at the last minute yelling, shouting insults at one another, Phil and David told them to keep moving. "Not much to choose between 'em, is there?" Phil said. "The little toffs with their ideas about privacy and these blokes."

By the time they got to Charing Cross, they had twenty minutes to catch the last train. They bribed the taxi driver to get them to King's Cross on time, then the men rushed to get tickets while Brenda and Dorothy, pushing luggage carts and encouraging Mrs Hutchison who was on the edge of fainting, hurried towards the train. It was a sleeper and they shouted at the conductor were there any berths left? The train was going in two minutes. He shouted back, "Get on, get on, farther down, farther down. Speak to the steward in Coach D."

"I can't go on," cried Mrs Hutchison, "I can't breathe!" Phil and David, waving tickets, came running alongside and scooped her up between them, ran with her, all of them (except Mrs Hutchison who was speechless) laughing as they ran.

A sweeper, an East Indian, began running beside them, shouting and shaking his broom.

"I am hoping you are kicked off this train. Kicked off. You coming at the last minute, expecting trains to wait for you, upsetting everyone. I jolly well hoping they kick you off."

They piled into the corridor of Coach D just before the train started to move. Phil and David went in search of the bedroom steward. "We'll see to you first," Brenda said.

Mrs Hutchison stood in the narrow passage and leaned her head against the cool window. The cleaner was running along beside the train, wild-eyed and shouting, brandishing his broom. She wanted to call out to him that he was mistaken, she wasn't like that at all, just tired and terribly ill. But when she opened her mouth to speak her voice was gone.

Compression

Compression

It was a game they had played last summer, driving along the narrow Cornish lanes, not in any particular hurry and with no specific destination except that they planned, eventually, to have a picnic on the moor. "St Tudy," Veronica said, "St Neot, St Breward, St Cleer. I've never heard of any of these saints."

"They must all be Cornish," her husband said, and asked if she had ever read bp Nichol's *The Martyrology*. That's how it started. ("St Art", she thought now, waiting for the Breakfast Special in Norma Jean's Restaurant; he would be the drawing master, in charge of illuminations, with St Ink, perhaps, as his assistant. She herself had been named not for the saintly Veronica and her hankie, but for Veronica Lake, her father's favourite movie actress in the 1940s.) That's how it started and once started, it was hard to stop. Okay, they would say to one another, that's enough; and then, over breakfast or in a pub or driving along in the rented car one or the other of them would get that silly smile and say, "St Ride, he looks after the horses." And the other would add, "along with St Able, he's the handyman about the place."

Waiting for her name to be called in the X-ray lab she had remembered St Agatha, a real saint, not one from their make-believe hagiography. St Agatha with her breasts on a platter holding her other symbol, the dreadful pincers which had cut them off; she hadn't seen until just now that St Agatha could also be part of their canon: St Ag, perhaps an irritable nun, a busybody. And then, because she had that sort of mind, a "stone-skipping mind" her husband called it ("St One," he suggested, "the big cheese. He even has it on his licence plate"), she thought to herself, *The Stag at Even,* remembering certain sepia-coloured prints in her grandfather's house. "St Ag at Even." What had St Agatha done to deserve such a terrible punishment? "St Ag at Bay."

Veronica was a woman who dealt with scarey situations by telling herself jokes or by talking too much. She had done both with the X-ray technician, a pleasant woman with upswept perfectly groomed blonde hair (a "bottle blonde" as Veronica's mother would have said). A friend had recently dyed her hair and Veronica almost didn't recognize her on the street.

"It's called 'integrating the grey,' " her friend said.

"Integrating the grey? I see little black hairs being bussed over to sit with little white hairs when you say that."

The X-ray technician was a fully integrated blonde. Veronica thought she looked more like the stereotype of a waitress than an X-ray technician.

"Hi, my name's Betty-Lou and today's special is . . ." But today's special was always the same at the Atomic-Paradise Café. And the waitress served you from a distance; she positioned you and instructed you to take a deep breath — hold it hold it — and then whirr whirr whirr — the machine took its picture and you were allowed to relax and breathe again.

"Have you ever had one of these?" Veronica asked.

"You know, I haven't. I suppose I should."

"My doctor was surprised that I'd never had one. That's why I'm here. There wasn't any lump, nothing like that; he just thought it would be a good idea." Veronica wanted to make it clear to this woman that there was nothing wrong, that she was only humouring her doctor. But to herself she sounded like one of those old jokes about Ann Landers; "Dear Ann Landers, I have a friend who is a homosexual, help me."

("St Ill. He runs the infirmary." "With some help from St Ick and St Op.")

"Terrify tissue," Veronica said, as the technician adjusted the machine and squashed Veronica's right breast into position.

"Pardon me?"

"Oh, it was a game we used to play when we were kids. You'd get a boy to spell out the words separately and then pronounce them. You'd challenge him, you and your girlfriend; you'd say, 'ha, I'll bet you can't spell terrify.' Of course he could. Then you'd do it again with tissue. He'd stand there, showing off, and after he'd spelt both words you'd say, 'now pronounce them.' He'd say, 'terrify tissue' and you'd say 'not at all.' You and your friend would collapse in giggles and shrieks and then run away."

"I don't get it," the technician said. "Terrify tissue?"

"Not at all."

"Oh, right." She smiled, "I'll have to remember that one." She brought the machine down against Veronica's breast.

"How's that?"

"Painful but bearable. I don't know why I thought of that old game. I suppose I was thinking about tissues and biopsies and I am terrified, I really am, in spite of the fact that I know this is just routine."

"There is no need to be," the technician said. "Nine times out of ten there's nothing wrong; if something does show up it usually turns out to be a cyst that can be aspirated in the specialist's office.''

''Aspirated?'' Veronica could feel herself sweating; the instructions had said not to use deodorant or talcum powder.

''He just draws out the fluid with a very long thin needle. It doesn't hurt.''

''How do you know? Has it been done to you? How could it — you haven't even had a mammogram.''

''I've seen it done.''

''Jesus,'' Veronica said, ''a long thin needle. Cross my heart and hope to die, stick a needle in my . . . We always x'd our heart with the St Andrew's cross, not up and down.''

''If you'll pull your left breast back as far as you can, count to three then take a deep breath and hold it. . . .'' The technician retreated to safety. ''One — two — three.''

Veronica inhaled. Gorilla-gram, balloon-o-gram, mammogram. It sounded like a telegram you might receive on Mother's Day. ''Happy Mother's Day from your left breast. Wish I was there.''

''Thanks,'' said the technician, ''just relax for a few minutes and we'll start on the other one.''

A month ago Veronica and her husband had been invited to a friend's fortieth birthday party. While people were finishing up at the buffet table a young man, who had been introduced as somebody's cousin who happened to be in town, stopped in front of the birthday girl (what did one say these days? Birthday woman? Birthday person? Celebrant?) and asked, ''Carole, do you remember me?''

''No,'' she said, smiling up at him (she was sitting in an armchair with a plate on her lap), ''no, I really don't.''

''Are you sure you don't remember me?''

''I'm sure.''

The women at the party looked at one another. He was incredibly handsome, with black hair and blue eyes. Not someone you'd forget.

He smiled, "Well, you're going to remember me." At which point he switched on a small tape recorder and began to dance.

The young man's crotch was just inches from Carole's face. And as he danced, he stripped — red leather tie — black silk shirt — black belt with silver buckle — black leather pants — until he was dancing there in this nice middle-class living-room dressed only in a black silk bikini. All the guests had stopped talking and eating and had come to watch. He danced in silence, except for the music. Danced with his eyes shut, completely self-absorbed. His chest was hairless except for two little rings of black hair around his nipples. I can't get no sat-is-fac-shun. Veronica looked up and saw Carole's children sitting at the top of the stairs, watching their mother's face. A stripogram. One of Carole's girlfriends had arranged it.

(St Rip would be in charge of the laundry room, mending sheets. Or did the members of the order sleep sheetless on mattresses stuffed with straw? St Raw — into self-flagellation.)

Whirr whirr whirr. "One more," said the technician, "and then we're done."

The beautiful young man in black. Death as a male stripper? Why not? "You're going to remember me." Not the grim reaper any more but a young actor-dancer between gigs.

He comes, not with a scythe but a portable tape-recorder.

Whirr whirr whirr. The machine peered into the depths of Veronica's left breast. Whirr whirr.

They rented the car at Heathrow and drove for a while in silence, still stunned by the long flight and the noise and

confusion of the airport. The original plan had been to
take the A4 to Bath, have tea there and then drop down
towards the southwest; but because they were so tired
they decided to get off the big motorways as soon as possible and take the slower, more scenic roads. And turned
the radio on just in time for the one o'clock news. A madman was loose in a town called Hungerford, gunning
down anybody in sight. A policeman had been shot, a
truck driver, and a teen-aged girl. Every hour on the hour
there was more news about the massacre, for that's what
they were calling it now, as the list of dead and wounded
climbed.

Veronica looked up Hungerford on the map. "If we
had gone to Bath," she said, "we might have stopped in
Hungerford for lunch."

Now the town was sealed off and the gunman holed up
in the local high school. Later there was news that a
woman had been shot dead in a nearby forest. Her
children were found by a grandmother taking a walk.
Next day in the papers it was reported that the little girl
had said, "A man in black shot my mummy. He has
taken the car keys. James and me cannot drive a car and
we are going home. We are tired."

By seven o'clock it was all over — the gunman had
shot himself — and they were approaching Dartmoor.
The last of the day's light lay in broad bright bands across
the west and a mist was rising. Just at the edge of the
moor a young man stood with a cardboard sign, hitchhiking.

They looked at one another.

"Not tonight," Veronica said, "I couldn't." She
switched off the radio.

Shapes formed out of the mist, dissolved back into it.
Pale ponies, sheep; dream animals made out of mist. She
felt vulnerable and afraid. Any minute now a figure
would step out into the middle of the road and hold up its
hand.

When they spoke at all, they spoke in whispers.

"If you will wait a few minutes in the other room," the technician said, "we'll just make sure the plates came out."

Veronica tied her smock. "Do men ever have mammograms?" she said.

"Occasionally."

"Do they have to sit out in that waiting room in pink smocks? It looks like a hairdressers out there — only nobody is holding a clipping of what they want to look like afterwards."

"We give the men white smocks, and we try to schedule them for 8 A.M. sharp."

"Sharp," Veronica said, with her hand on the doorknob, "Do they mind you touching them?"

She laughed. "Only if my hands are cold. No, it's some of the women who mind, particularly the older ones. They don't like another woman touching their breasts."

"Probably the same women who would never go to a 'lady doctor.' My mother is one of those."

"If you'll just wait a few minutes; this won't take long."

Back in the outer room Veronica leafed through magazines. There ought to be generic waiting-room magazines, she thought. People only pretend to read in places like this. At the back of a *Better Homes and Gardens* she found an ad for a thing called a "Bosom Buddy" — something you could stick in your bra if one of your breasts had been sliced off. Money-back guarantee. No one would ever know.

So long as you kept your clothes on. So long as your husband didn't leave you. How to explain to the new boyfriend? And where? In the restaurant over coffee and dessert? In the car? In the bedroom? Put on a record of Willie Nelson singing "All of Me" and make a big joke of it. "Darling, there's less to this than meets the eye."

"Ma Ma," the breast, a doublet, like what it signifies. And "papa" also, probably not referring to Daddy at all but to the tit. She had had rivers of milk, torrents. The milk rushing in when the baby cried was the most erotic feeling she had ever known.

Did whales get cancer? Cats? Dogs? Sheep? Did monkeys get it? Did apes? Cancer. An ugly word. It began with a shape like a sickle or a breast with a big bite out.

("St Oops," said her husband, "the clumsy one."

"St Ring," she offered, "in charge of the bells."

"St Rand, sent away for dirty habits."

"Along with St Rut and St Rumpet.")

The aide called her name. Veronica stood up and started towards the changing room. The aide shook her head.

"Would you mind going down the hall for a few more pictures please."

"Why? What's the matter?" Her voice came out too loud. One of the other women looked up but quickly returned to her magazine.

"If you would just go down to the last room on your right. The technician will be with you shortly." She frowned at her list and called another name. A very young woman stood up.

The single waitress in Norma Jean's Restaurant was Vietnamese, no doubt one of the boat people. Her face seemed wiped clean of emotion, neither friendly nor unfriendly. What had this woman seen? What might she have suffered on her voyage to freedom? Sharks, pirates, rape, death, disease? Veronica tried to imagine the various levels of hell this woman might have travelled through in order to get here today, safe, in a clean uniform, with a steady wage. She called back the orders in her own language — perhaps the cook was her husband. Veronica asked if it was too late for the Breakfast Special. It was an old-fashioned coffee-shop, with maroon padded booths and Formica tables, plastic-covered menus. Today's special was "beef live with onions," typed on a little strip of paper.

("St Eel, the fisherman."

"St Umble, speaks in a whisper, always genuflecting."

"St Y, the one who asks too many questions.")

The woman from Hungerford had taken her children on a picnic. It was just one of those horrible coincidences that she stumbled upon the madman's secret place. When a small black-and-white dog, followed by a man in corduroys, cut across the place where Veronica and her husband were picnicking up against the ruins of a great gaunt engine house, she had to keep herself from screaming.

"It's all right," her husband said quietly. "Just a man and his dog out for a walk. Relax."

"I don't think I shall ever feel quite the same about picnics in the country," Veronica said. She patted the dog, ashamed that her hand was shaking.

"It's all *right*," her husband said again.

"I should have known," Veronica said, "I never liked that one as much as the other. The sinister breast. Okay, what happens now?"

"We take more pictures. You probably moved."

"And then?"

"And then your doctor will get in touch with you in a few days."

"And what if there is something?"

"Then he'll probably send you for an ultrasound."

"And then?"

"Well, that gives a much clearer reading. As I said before, these little things are usually cysts."

"Nine times out of ten."

"Yes."

"And they aspirate it," Veronica drew out the 's,' "with a long, thin needle."

"Yes."

As she walked back down the hall to the elevator she imagined all the frightened people behind the closed doors, leafing through magazines, waiting for their names to be called. This was a huge building, fifteen stories high. She thought she could smell fear in the halls, a sharp foxy smell that made you wrinkle your nose in disgust.

When the waitress in Norma Jean's Restaurant brought her order, the Breakfast Special, juice, coffee and a single poached egg on toast, Veronica stared at it and then pushed it away. ''Trust me,'' she thought. She went to the back and paid her bill and left. The waitress looked at her but made no comment.

As she stood waiting for the bus Veronica thought again of St Agatha at Even, imagined her alone on a darkening moor somewhere, weeping, cursing, howling, holding out her poor, sad breasts to the indifferent moon, her black shawl flapping around her and the chill mists rising.

Blue
Spanish Eyes

Blue
Spanish Eyes

Over and over the same question: relatives, friends, husbands and wives at breakfast tables on both sides of the Atlantic. Why? Examining the blurry photos again. A sensible woman, a grandmother, staring straight at the camera with an open, friendly smile. Then, further down, the Identikit drawing — HAVE YOU SEEN THIS MAN?

Her daughter wept, her sons. Why? When? (remembering all the warnings about strangers). Why? And where was she now?

She cannot answer, of course, for her mouth is stopped up with mud.

I first saw him in the concourse of the Inverness Railway Station, a tall young man leaning over his bike, trying to catch his breath. His T-shirt was soaked with sweat so that the vertebrae underneath stuck up prominently, almost as though they were buttons, as though he had been buttoned neatly into his skin.

"Tender buttons," I thought, but Stein meant

mushrooms, not the backbone of a bicycle-rider. The arc
of his back and the wheels of his cycle made a nice com-
position; I wished I were a photographer so that I could
approach him and ask if he'd mind if I took his picture — no, don't look up, you're perfect the way you
were. But I don't take photographs, just snapshots of my
children and their children — a snapshot is quite a different thing from a photograph. I don't carry a camera
when I'm travelling, not because I fear it might get stolen
but because I fear I might stop looking. However, once in
a while I regret this policy and now was one of those
times.

The high arc of the boy's back, his stillness (except for
the deep breaths, in/out, in/out, in/out), the back of his
neck which was tanned and freckled by the sun. He had
dark red hair, the colour of an Irish setter, but were I a
photographer I would have taken his photograph in black
and white. In the beginning, then, he was just an
aesthetic arrangement for me — like Whistler's mother.

I had been a week up in the Orkney Islands, walking
and sightseeing. The weather was perfect except for one
day of rain, and the Orkneys had impressed and moved
me in curious ways. The whole place is a kind of museum
and yet the people go about their daily lives in a completely natural way, in spite of the standing stones and
Viking graves and neolithic treasures, many no doubt still
to be uncovered. In the small museum at the Tomb of the
Eagles I was allowed to hold in my hands the skull of a
woman who died over four thousand years ago. The skull
was the colour of field mushrooms, smooth and slightly
cool to the touch.

She died at thirty-four, an old woman for those times.
There was a deep indentation across the top of her head
where a band of leather had pressed down, day after day,
year after year, as she carried her loads from one place to
another. I held the skull to my ear, like a shell as though I
might hear her calling to me over all those centuries. Her

back molars had been worn down by chewing, softening leather perhaps. The farmer's wife, who ran the museum, smiled at me. ''We are all Chalk Thompson's bairns.''

''I'm sorry?''

''An old name for Death,'' she said, and took the skull from me to give to the next person in our group.

Fat sheep nibble at the grass around the headstones in the cemetery at Orphir. A farmer digs a hole to bury a cow and turns up a Viking skeleton. But it wasn't a morbid or dreary place; I wouldn't want to give the wrong impression. There was just a certain acceptance of it all that left me feeling cleansed, uplifted, more at peace than I had been in a long long time.

When I travel I wear my wedding ring and if the subject comes up I say my husband has passed on. I don't add that he passed on to a younger woman. There's no shame in being divorced these days, not like when I was growing up, but a widow is a highly respectable thing to be. I figure my husband owes me that, my little deceit. I feel safer as a widow than a divorcée; a widow, unlike a widower, isn't necessarily looking for another mate. And if someone asks, ''when did you lose your husband?'' I can answer in all honesty.

I had reserved a seat on the 5:30 train from Inverness to Edinburgh just in case the train from the north was late; as a result I had plenty of time on my hands, although not quite enough to venture too far away from the city centre. I put my bag in a locker and walked around a bit, browsed in a couple of touristy shops which sold the usual tartan ties and kilts, lambswool sweaters, shortbread, whisky miniatures and silver jewellery based on Celtic designs; but I had already done my shopping in Orkney and had it sent home, so I soon tired of that. It was tea-time, but the one tea-room I really liked the look of was full up so I retraced my steps and had an indifferent tea at the Station Hotel. Nearly everything had been eaten up except for some dry cheese-and-tomato rolls and packet biscuits. I had a Scottish mother who always stopped for tea and whose love of baking would be frowned upon by any self-respecting dietitian today. We had cream scones and pancakes and shortbread (with real butter) and Dundee cake and maid of honour tarts and Victoria sandwich. Thursday was her baking day and I raced home to lick bowls and munch on pastry strips which had been sprinkled with cinnamon and sugar and baked in a hot, hot oven. My mother laughed at her excesses, and blamed it on the war, even though, after she met my American father, her family had more than most. My father says she fell in love with him on the day a huge fruitcake arrived from his relatives in Massachusetts. My father was tall and skinny, like this boy with the bicycle. He could eat and eat and never gain an ounce. My mother was short and rather plain and grew stout as the years went on. At the age of fifteen, realizing that I took more after my mother's side than my Yankee father's, I gave up all the sweets. My mother laughed at me and went right on baking. She was a great hit with my boyfriends and, later, with my children. Now that she is dead I have begun to bake, with recipes from her old black-covered notebook. I take boxes of goodies to my father and I bake for various groups I belong to. No doubt, when my grandson has graduated from baby food I shall bake — I would have baked — for him too, secretly of course; his mother never touches sugar. My father teases her and sings an old song his father taught him, something about everything being "illegal or immoral or it makes you fat."

I looked at the station clock and went to retrieve my suitcase. When I came back the boy — the young man — was over at the fruit stand very carefully selecting fruit for the trip. He pointed here and there and made the seller laugh. I smiled because I knew exactly what he was doing. The price of fruit in Scotland always shocks me; I too am very picky here as I want to make sure I get my money's worth. We are spoiled back home; I've tried to imagine what it was like during the war, with an ounce of this and an ounce of that, one egg a week. I was only a toddler when the war ended and we left for the United States. The first time I came back I thought some miracle would happen and all my infant memories would present themselves to me like old home movies; it wasn't so. I felt comfortable in Scotland, that was the extent of it. (But not comfortable with my relatives, those stern, uncompromising Presbyterians. I stayed at a Bed and Breakfast in Edinburgh and took the bus out to visit those that were left. Two of my ancient aunties bragged that they had never been below the border. No central heating to this day and fires not lit until November.)

The young man turned quickly and saw me smiling. He paid for his purchases, stuffed them in his backpack and came over, pushing the bike with one hand. That was the first I had a good look at his face. He stood looking down at me with a cheeky grin.

"And just what are you smiling at?" he said.

Once, on a beach in Crete, a woman from the American south asked me if I liked lookin' at all those little no-hipped boys in their tiny swimsuits. She was about fifteen years older than I was, about the age I was that day in Inverness.

"No," I said, "not particularly." She wiggled her painted toes.

"Well, Sugar, you got that pleasure comin' to you."

But it wasn't like that at all, it never has been for me. I look at mouths and eyes. It's the head that's important, like the engine at the front of a train. For me, usually, the rest of the body is just pulled along by the head. And this boy's body was nothing to write home about in any case. When he was actually in motion he seemed more than loose-limbed, dangerously so, as though he needed to be re-strung. An arm or a leg might come flying off at any minute. But his eyes: his eyes were a bright, clear, cloudless blue. I felt that if his eyes were sliced open the blue colour would go all the way through, like the yolk of a hard-boiled egg, that eyes such as those could not possibly be hollow. "Blue Spanish Eyes," I thought, although he was as Scottish as they come.

"I was smiling at the way you chose your purchases," I said. "I do the same thing. I want *this* particular banana, *that* apple."

He sat down next to me on one of the ugly plastic chairs British Rail now provides for its customers. I suppose they are easy to keep clean but I would prefer old-fashioned waiting-rooms and wooden benches. Even Waverley Station, that opulent place, has these seats which belong only at some fast-food outlet. His legs were much too long for him to sit comfortably in such chairs.

"New England," he said, "but with a touch of something else." Here he launched into a clever parody of the Kennedys. "Ask what you can do for your country," he said. "Hahvahd Yahd."

"I don't talk like that," I said, "do I?"

"No, not really, but it's there. What else? Want to hear my New York accent, hey youse, want to hear dat? Or my Georgia accent, won't yawl have a bit of Mama's peach pickle? You name it, I can do it."

"Are you an actor?" I asked. He didn't seem like an actor, less self-absorbed, although he looked a bit like Gregory in *Gregory's Girl*.

"Me! An actor? Not on your life. But I can do a great Marlon Brando. Want to see Marlon Brando play Hamlet?" He rolled up the sleeve of his T-shirt and tucked away an imaginary pack of cigarettes.

"To be or not to be," he growled. Then held the pose, head on one side.

I waited.

"That's it," he said. "Pretty good, hey? No, I'm not an actor, just a film junkie. Especially the old films. Especially films in the afternoon. I dropped out of school so I could go to films in the afternoon. My mother never knew until she ended up sitting next to me one afternoon. And then wasn't there hell to pay, oh my.''

''I have to go now,'' I said, ''my train's just been put up on the board.''

''Edinburgh?''

''That's right.''

''I'm going as far as Stirling. Could I sit with you? I promise to be entertaining.''

''I reserved a seat,'' I said, ''the seats around me might be taken.''

''We'll see about that. Just let me put my bicycle in the guard's van and I'll come find you.'' He paused. ''That is, if you're agreeable?''

I'd finished all the books I'd brought with me, except a P.D. James I was really saving for the plane and some ladies magazine I had bought just for amusement. Having someone to talk to for three hours on a Sunday afternoon might be fun. Or listen to. I wasn't sure how much talking I would manage to get in. I strapped my bag onto the little wheeled cart I had vowed ten years ago I would never own. A wheeled cart seemed in the same category with Oil of Olay or even those plastic raincaps old ladies carry in their purses to protect their perms if it should rain. The boy had loped on ahead. Perhaps I would be seated and my luggage stowed away by the time he found me. I could always tell him about hitchhiking around Europe with an enormous pack when I was his age or even a little younger. It was borrowed and the base hit my spine in the wrong place. They weren't rip-stop nylon then either; they were heavy brown canvas, leather and metal. When I got to the train and was walking along the platform searching for my car, I decided to make a game out of the wheelie I was dragging behind me. Just in case he was watching. ''Come along, Shep,'' I said, ''there's a good dog.'' But I was settled and reading a magazine before he finally slid into the empty seat across from me.

"The Lady," he said, plucking it out of my hands and flipping through the pages.

" ' "I'll never forget," says Jeanne Laidlaw, recalling her WARTIME CHILDHOOD.' Is this what you read? 'Fitted bed linens.' 'The Brightest Idea in Kitchen Boards.' 'Society for the Assistance of Ladies in Reduced Circumstances.' Are you looking for a position as a nanny or a resident housekeeper in a nursing home? You don't really seem the type."

"I bought them as a joke — to take back home. I didn't know magazines like this still existed. *Woman's Own*, sure, but not *The Lady*."

He tossed the magazines aside and took out a pack of cards.

When someone you love tells you that it's over, when you've been married to that someone for twenty years, something terrible and permanent happens to you. It's like being in a bad car crash or an airplane crash. Even if you survive, even if you survive with no visible scars, something happens to your soul. You become frightened of things that never frightened you before — loud noises, a sudden scream, the sight of blood. You have lost a certain innocence, or perhaps the word is "trust." You never get over it; all you can do is get around it.

Even when he says you've done nothing wrong, that it's he who is at fault. Even when he says there's no particular other woman, just a desire to "explore other avenues of myself." It is probably easier if there is another woman, a name, perhaps a face. Then the hurt and anger can be localized, contained, instead of spread wide, like an oil spill. It spreads to strangers, even to this boy. What would he think of me for having a wheelie, for buying such a stupid, conservative magazine? What would he think of me when I told him I don't play cards? I watched his strong hands shuffle the pack and then reshuffle. The hairs on his arms were like gold wires. I noticed then that he wore a wedding ring.

"The only game I know," I said, "is gin rummy. Other than children's games, snap or go-fish — games like that."

"Just choose a card," he said, "any card. Memorize it and stick it back in the deck." He smiled. His face was covered in faint freckles, as though he'd been dusted with some spice. I hesitated.

"Hurry along," he said, "we've not got all day."

The city of Inverness stands at the top of the Great Glen, a geological fault that slices at a diagonal across the Highlands. When the Caledonian Canal was built in the early-nineteenth century the North Sea was connected to the Atlantic Ocean. In nature great faults are seen as challenges — at least to engineers. Things are made to link up by bridges, canals and other ingenious devices. My husband was an engineer, his heroes were — no doubt still are — Thomas Telford and Isambard Kingdom Brunel. He was "handy," as they say over here and could fix anything. Except our marriage. Marriages wear out, he said, just like motorcars; it isn't anything you've done.

(I memorized the Creed at my mother's knee: We have left undone those things which we ought to have done and done those things which we ought not to have done and there is no health in us.)

Of course the boy picked the right card, again and again. His fingers danced above the little table which lay between us.

"You're a teacher, I'll wager," he said.

"A professor of Art History."

He pulled a face.

"A *professor*, is it? Good pay? Long holidays? Lots of trips to places with *objets d'art*? The Mona Lisa. Venus de Milo, that sort of thing?"

"Are you mocking me?"

"Not really. I believe in education. Or I do now. There was a while when I was one of the lost boys — you know — Peter Pan. Didn't want to grow up and face responsibility.''

He made a waterfall of the cards, and then another. A thick honey-coloured light lay over the purple hills.

''How old do you think I am?'' he said.

''Twenty-five.''

He looked at me in surprise. ''Bang on.''

''I have a son the same age as you.''

''What's his name?'' He held out the deck and I took another card.

''Donald,'' I said, ''after his grandfather.'' Those blue eyes watching me, not the cards.

''That's my name too,'' he said. ''Do you think we were fated to meet?''

He gave me a smile of such incredible sweetness I could have wept. Men my age did not smile at me like that, openly, just delighting in the moment, the coincidence.

''His grandfather was a Scot,'' I said.

''My Mother was a Scot — from Fife.''

'' 'The thane of Fife had a wife: where is she now?' You see, I remember something from all that Shakespeare at school. That's what I heard in your voice, then, an echo of Fife.''

''And you are from Glasgow,'' I said, ''or thereabouts.''

He put the cards away and we began to talk, really talk, as the daylight faded and the train rattled along in the dusk. Every so often I wondered if my sons — either of them — would have talked so openly to a strange woman of my age. Students talk to me sometimes, it's true. Young people like to talk to you, Mother, my daughter said once. I wanted to tell her — even your father, when he was young.

The boy — Donald — had been married for three months; his wife taught maths at a secondary school. He bought her a bike for a wedding present and they went cycling in the Western Isles. It was brilliant, that trip, he said, rolling his *r*'s.

"Why does that make you cry?" he said, and put his hand over mine.

He went to the buffet car and got us each a drink. In the Ladies my cheeks were pink, as though I had a fever.

His grandmother died in July and he still couldn't think of her without becoming tearful. His grandmother! How could you not trust someone who talked so about his grandmother?

I was twice his age and yet we had both read all of Robert Louis Stevenson, most of Poe, Jack London, the Swallows and Amazons books.

"Your hair is a lovely colour," he said.

"I help it along a bit now," I said. "It was a lovely colour on its own not long ago."

He was studying to be an electrical engineer and every so often he was sent, by the firm, up to a place beyond Inverness. He always took his bike. On the classified pages of *The Lady* he drew diagrams, trying earnestly to explain exactly what it was he did up there. I watched his hands with their freckled backs.

"When do you leave for home?" he said, without looking up from his elaborate drawings of circuits.

"That stuff's lost on me," I said, "I couldn't get beyond algebra and Train A and Train B heading towards each other at different speeds — when would they crash." I wanted him to look up, to look at me with his blue Spanish eyes, but he continued drawing.

"Next week," I said, "But before that I'm treating myself to a room at the North British Hotel so I can walk around Princess Gardens looking at all the free Fringe events."

"Ah, the pull of the city, the crowds, the grease-paint. I can understand that. But you shouldn't turn your back on the mountains so soon. Have you never explored the Grampians or the Cairngorms?"

Now he looked at me and put the pencil down.

When he suggested I get off at Kingussie and spend another day or two in the mountains I nodded and thanked him for his advice. Why not, I thought, why not? At the station he handed me down my bag and my wheeled cart, kissed me. Have you ever held your hand over a candle flame? He wished me *bon voyage*.

The taxi driver took me to a small hotel where I asked for a room at the front. Then I went upstairs, had a sweet, slow bath and changed my clothes. I sang in the bathtub: "please please don't cry. This is just adios and not good-bye." I sang the song all the way through and then I started again. Blue Spanish eyes, dum dum de dum de dum of Mexico. I told the landlady my son was on a cycling tour and perhaps he would join me later. I saw him from the upstairs window and ran down to meet him.

Late that night we went for a walk beyond the town. A gentle rain was falling, more like a cool web than any rain I had ever felt before. The air smelled of rain and of heather.

Then the rain stopped and he took my hand.

"See," he said, "even the moon is lying on her back."

That was the first of several lovely days we spent in that wild country.

Sunday Morning,
June 4, 1989

Sunday Morning,
June 4, 1989

Both Pauline and her new boyfriend like to sleep on the
far side of the bed, the side nearest the door; Pauline, in
case she wants to get up in the night and pee,
Richard — he says — so that he would be more easily
able to confront a burglar. Pauline thinks it's more likely
that he is not used to staying the entire night with his current loved one. So when the telephone rings in what
seems to be the middle of the night (4:45 by the bedside
clock) she is glad she is sleeping alone. Crawling over the
body of a new boyfriend, a new "beau," as her mother
would say, would be awkward and embarrassing for the
crawler and no doubt annoying to the crawlee. He might
think he was being attacked.

"Pauline?" For a few seconds she does not recognize
the almost-man voice of her youngest nephew, who in the
space of a year and a half, has grown eight inches and instructed the family that henceforth, his name is Charlie,
not Chunky. Not Chunky ever again.

"Charlie? Is something wrong? Have you any idea
what time it is out here? Even the early bird is still asleep,

as is the early worm. What's the matter? Where's your dad?''

''Dad and Gillian are in London, remember? Second honeymoon combined with business. Gillian took a new nightgown and her lap-top. They left last night. But Dad asked me to call you and it's cheaper before eight. The Ayatollah is freaking out again. He thinks it might be serious this time.''

The Ayatollah is Pauline and her brother's name for their difficult mother. Sometimes they call her the One True Cross. They use these names all the time between themselves but somehow it bothers her when she hears such disrespect from the lips of a nineteen-year-old — even if he does have a moustache.

''She's your grandmother, Charlie. I think perhaps you shouldn't call her that.''

''Whatever.'' She knows he thinks she's being a typical adult-hypocrite. ''Anyway, he wants you to talk to her but don't say he told you to, okay? And he's left a number where he can be reached if you need him.''

Pauline searches for a pencil, writes down the number in London, and hangs up. It's far too early to call her mother, who is ninety-two and has difficulty getting to sleep; so she makes a pot of coffee and takes it back to bed with her. She dozes a little and waits for the clock-radio to come on at 6 A.M. Another thing she can't do if Richard sleeps over — she likes to hear the early-morning news before she gets up. Sometimes news items actually become part of her dreams. Pauline works as a secretary for a mental health team and is very interested in dreams. As she sips her coffee she wonders if her desire to be around mental health experts has anything to do with the long history of her mother's aberrations. Both Pauline and her brother, Nick, are of the opinion that their mother, who waited to have children until she was thirty-nine and forty, suffered a post-partum depression from which she never recovered. Nowadays, she could

have sought help, but back then it was grin and bear it.
Or don't grin and bear it.

"Dad said that if she ends up in the funny farm, she
has only herself to blame." Charlie had sounded just like
Nick as he said this.

"Oh really," Pauline said. "When you are a bit older
you will know how seldom a disturbed person has only
themself to blame. And your father certainly knows better
than that."

"I think he's just fed up. She always does this
whenever he plans a vacation."

Nick was an economist and taught at Syracuse University. Gillian was his second wife, also an economist.
Pauline was not fond of Gillian, who seemed to her too
"kittenish," too coy and flirtatious. But she had to hand
it to her — Gillian was very good with the old lady, did
up picnic hampers with Hallmark plates and napkins and
fancy finger-foods, and took them to the Oneonta Senior
Citizens' Complex where their mother lived, spending
entire Sunday afternoons looking at photo albums or
coaxing her mother-in-law out for a little walk. Pauline
got glowing descriptions of Gillian's visits in her mother's
letters. Every item of food was listed, down to what kind
of bread or rolls and whether white or brown. Nick was
good to his mother too, of course, and visited her regularly, as did Charlie, but Gillian was the star. Last month,
on her annual trip east, Pauline, Nick, Gillian and
Charlie had all taken the old woman out to dinner at the
Carriage House. Her mother had cranberry juice
cocktail, at Gillian's suggestion ("Remember how you
enjoyed it last time?") Later on in the meal, her mother
said, "How come you've all got such pretty glasses and
mine's just plain? Could be a kitchen glass, couldn't it?"
Gillian signalled the waitress and asked if it would be
possible to have the prettier glass on this special occasion.
All the others, including Charlie, were drinking alcohol;
no doubt juice came in plain glasses. Children drank

juice. But if Mother could find some way of feeling slighted, she would. Perhaps, when Gillian had been in the family for several years, she would not be so accommodating. Gillian never referred to their mother as the Ayatollah. She called her Vivian and seemed genuinely to like her.

When the six o'clock news came on, Pauline, who had gone to bed at a reasonable hour the night before and had not listened to the radio past ten, heard the first reports of the killings in Tiananmen Square and the death of the real Ayatollah, Khomeini. She carried her small transistor into the bathroom. Over the noise of the water running into the tub, she heard the words "blood bath." A reporter was describing the massacre of the Chinese protesters.

"Fascists! Fascists!" a Chinese student was yelling. The People's Army had turned against the people. Her mother's problems, whatever they were this time — something to do with the annual inspection, Charlie had said, something to do with an accusation that the top of the stove wasn't clean enough, that powder was spilled on the bathroom floor — seemed so unimportant compared to what was going on in the rest of the world that Pauline had a strong urge not to phone her mother at all. But as she had learned, you can't get rid of people, especially parents, by declaring them over — or putting a country and a continent between you. At 9:30 A.M., Pacific Time, she looked up her mother's number and dialled. She left the radio on, tuned to "Sunday Morning," and a CBS reporter was yelling, hysterically — "Watch out, over there on the left! They're coming this way — no, no, I'm not going to stay here and get shot at!" More gunfire and the tape went dead as her mother picked up the phone.

"Hello, Mother, it's Pauline."

"Pauline?" Pause. "Pauline, how are you?" Her mother's voice sounded so thin and old, it was like the voices on the cylindrical records her grandfather had let her listen to on rainy Sunday afternoons. It was like the voice of someone from another dimension, frail, papery, an old leaf speaking.

"I'm fine, Mother, how are you?" There was a long silence and then that quavering voice again.

"Pauline, when you went to New York before coming here, did you go for a medical check-up?"

"No. Why would I go to New York for a medical check-up? We have doctors up here in Canada you know. Specialists even. It's not just igloos and Mounties."

"What? I didn't get the last bit." Her mother was quite deaf and needed a new hearing aid. Pauline had offered to buy her one, but no.

"Never mind, Mother. I didn't go to New York for a medical check-up. I don't need a medical check-up. Why would you think that?" She was practically shouting, but still she could hear the sound of gunfire and the cries of the Chinese. Real gunfire didn't sound as impressive as the gunfire used in radio dramas. More like firecrackers. Unless you happened to be there. Pauline had never seen anyone shot point blank or corpses with their heads cut off — except in the papers.

"I don't know. When you were here you seemed rather subdued. Not your usual self. I thought maybe you were down in the dumps about something."

Pauline wondered if her mother would recognize her "usual self" if it walked up to her on the street. How the hell would she know what was her, Pauline's, "usual self"? But now she had her entrance cue and she picked it up.

"No, I'm not down in the dumps, Mother. Are you down in the dumps?"

Long pause. Her mother was crying. Finally, "I don't think I can talk about it. I think I'd better hang up."

"Don't hang up, Mother." She pictured her mother standing there in her aqua dressing-gown, talking on the telephone to a daughter who lived thousands of miles away. Nick and Gillian thousands of miles away as well.

"Charlie was coming out this afternoon with his new girlfriend, but I called and told him not to come, I'm too upset for visitors."

"Can you tell me what's upset you Mother?"

Chinese students in Canada were being interviewed. Some of them were weeping openly. Some had visas that were running out — they sounded afraid. Pauline sometimes joked with her friends that she was the only kid on the block whose mother never said, "Eat up, think of the starving people in China." "My mother," (she would say at dinner parties, being amusing) "my mother wouldn't have minded if they'd all starved. Had she thought of it she probably would have said, 'eat up, have more, so there will be less for the starving people in China.' "

"Pauline!" her friends would say, "you're awful."

"But it's true," she said, laughing, "you can't exactly accuse her of discrimination since she is absolutely democratic in her hatred of foreigners — she hates them all. It is foreigners who have caused the decline of America in case you didn't know."

"I don't think I can talk right now." Whatever the problem, her mother's struggle against complete breakdown was obviously real.

"Perhaps you could write me about it. Could you do that?" Her mother was a compulsive letter-writer. Years ago, when Pauline had been afraid of her mother, the letters would sometimes sit for a week before she could get up the courage to open them and confront the latest accusation or grievance. Pauline saw them as letter-bombs, ticking away in the desk drawer . . . tick-tick-tick. Whoever made up that children's chant about sticks and stones can break my bones but names can never hurt me had not met Pauline's mother.

"I don't think you read my letters," her mother said now. Could her mother read minds?

"Of course I do." (Now)

"You don't answer my questions."

"What questions are these?"

"It doesn't matter."

Pauline examined her toenails, which last night she had painted a bright red, in honour of summer's arrival on the Coast. Fire-engine red, Chinese red.

When she had been a teenager, Revlon had come out with a bright red which proved very popular for lips and nails. It was called "Fire and Ice." Now Pauline wonders if some advertising copywriter with an Arts degree had thought that up, remembering Frost's poem of that name, if not the poem itself.

Pauline liked that bright, clear, glossy red. She no longer wore lipstick at all but she still bought red shoes and painted bits of furniture with red lacquer. Even her kitchen door. To the Chinese, red was the colour of good fortune. When a new store opened in Chinatown, you would see floral arrangements decorated with red ribbons printed with Chinese characters in gold. Last weekend she and Richard had gone for dim sum in Chinatown. Pauline liked the noisy friendliness of Chinese restaurants and all the large round tables full of families. Both she and Richard had grown children studying or working in other provinces or overseas. None in China, Thank God.

Pauline herself had always wanted to go to China, not to visit but to stay for at least a year. Even an old MA in English would probably get her a teaching job. She had worked for the Peace Corps in Ghana, before she became completely disillusioned with America and moved, with her new and equally disillusioned husband, to Canada. They had accidentally been assigned to share a house outside Kumasi and had ended up getting married. The relationship had always been more comfortable and friendly than wildly passionate; but then one day he had fallen madly in love with the young woman who sold them coffee every Saturday and that was that. Pauline was surprised and shocked at how devastated she felt and still continues to feel. Although she is unaware of it, she still, after ten years, compares most men to her ex, who is an historian of some repute, specializing in the history of the Sikhs in Canada. Or that's what he did specialize in. He now plans to take early retirement and work in Nicaragua with his wife. Pauline tries to be amusing about this too. "Nee-har-wa-wa," she says. "You have to be sure you pronounce it properly or you're not really politically correct." Pauline has told her ex, whose name is Phil, that she thinks his future plan is a cop-out, that his knowledge of the Sikhs could be a big help in such a prejudiced province as B.C. He ought to stay home. However, he has two more years until he retires at fifty-five. Maybe, he'll change his mind or maybe Sonia will have a baby. Anything can happen in two years. Or even overnight.

"Pauline?" her mother is saying.

"Yes Mother, I'm here."

"I thought maybe you had hung up on me."

"No, no, I'm here." Not that she wouldn't like to. Hang up. But she could no more walk away from her mother than she could walk away from the woman in the mirror. The woman in the mirror simply waited for your return.

"They're trying to get me out," her mother said, "me and Harriet." Harriet was the middle-aged woman who came in and "did" for her mother once a week. She was not the woman the Senior Citizens' Complex, a church-run organization, recommended, but she did have some vague tie with the Methodist church. Harriet had developed high blood pressure and was slowing down, but she listened to Pauline's mother and did the laundry. She was probably her mother's only regular confidante.

"Who are 'they'?"

"The social worker and the inspector. They're all worried about HUD, you see, because HUD's cracking down

on these places and they — the people here — use un-
trained staff from the church. They're not supposed to do
that. So of course they're anxious and want everything
spic and span when the HUD people come around.''

Pauline tried to remember what HUD was, if she had
ever known, but all she could think of was Paul Newman.
Housing and something development? How Utterly
Dreary? Help Urban Developers? Her mother could
hardly speak. Great jagged pauses and the sound of sobs.

''The inspector said there was grease on top of my
stove, and that social worker came out of the bathroom
and said, 'The bathroom's dirty.' I had spilled some ep-
som salts in the corner and I guess Harriet hadn't seen it.
She has a bad leg you know and can't work as well as she
used to. I tried to explain but of course they wouldn't
listen. They want to get rid of her — and me too. And the
office sends around forms every year, do you need
repairs? Well I wrote yes, because the catch doesn't work
on the balcony door — it doesn't close properly. They
sent workmen, young fellows. In and out — they have
skeleton keys you know — they can come in anytime they
like and they did, without knocking even. They took
hours. I was so exhausted I had to go to sleep all afternoon!''

The sound of her mother's weeping mingles with the
sound of lamentation on the radio. Ululating — how did
the women do that? Mourning the loss of their leader.
What had the Ayatollah ever done for those women?

''Did you complain?'' Pauline says now.

''I wouldn't dare. I'd be out on the street tomorrow.''

''Oh come!''

''Oh yes I would. Years ago, when I first came here,
there were bugs in the cupboards. I suppose the concrete
hadn't cured or something. An old lady three doors down
complained and when they didn't pay attention she wrote
a letter to the State Board of Health. She was out as quick

as you can say Jack Robinson. And she was practically at death's door. They said that's why she had to go — if you get sick you're out — but we knew better.''

Pauline wonders what death's door looks like. Black, no doubt, with possibly a fanlight, like a door in a Georgian crescent. Tasteful. But the truth was that Death came knocking at your door, whatever colour it was. Or didn't bother to knock, just opened your door with a skeleton key ha ha. Pauline thought of a joke that once made the rounds of her grade three class. ''What do baby ghosts call their parents?'' ''Dead and Mummy.'' Funny then. Death seems very remote if one is in grade three. She tries to think what she can do to help her mother, who is old, who is lonely, who has never ever been able to make friends, who has a genius in the other direction. For making enemies. But had looked so well on Pauline's recent visit. Well and more or less content. Her mother's voice seemed to gain strength now that she'd been able to say what was troubling her.

''He was Armenian, you know, the fellow who started this place. His son is the manager now. Smart as a whip the old man was. But nice. He was always nice to me. He heard that the state was going to give money for senior citizens' homes and he got right in there on the ground floor. That was twenty years ago. Those Armenians are smart you know. They buy up real estate and develop it. Do you remember that tailor back home, the one you used to like to go to down by the Arlington Hotel. That's what he did. Bought up a lot of real estate on the East Side and made a fortune. He was an Armenian.''

''No,'' Pauline says, ''I don't remember him.'' But that's not quite true. His daughter was in her class at school, a sharp-featured, hooked-nosed, black-haired girl who wore exquisite but unsuitable dresses. The other girls were mean to her and said she looked like a witch. Now Pauline is surprised to hear that her mother has a good word to say about the Armenians — any foreigners. She wants to ask her mother if she knows where ''Armenia'' is, what does she think of recent events in Azerbaijan for instance, but that would be mean.

Pauline's mother has recently changed her will, much to the amusement of the rest of the family. She had planned to leave her body to the Harvard Medical School but now she has taken it back. In a recent letter she informed Pauline of this and explained that doctors in the States seemed to be on such a joy-ride these days with organ transplants and all that she didn't want to think of her eyes looking out of some Puerto Rican face. All this welfare and health care for people who couldn't even speak English was ruining Medicare for people like herself. Now she wanted to be cremated.

Her mother had begun to cry again and the radio program had moved on to a big AIDS conference in Montreal. She wanted to shout at her mother to get off the phone and turn on the television for Christ's sake, have a look at the larger pain and misery in the world. She wanted to ask, Mother, have you ever risked your life? But her mother's personal misery was what was real to her.

''Pauline! I don't want to go to a Home!''

''Don't worry Mother, you won't.'' Hush, hush, there, there. How real was the possibility of her mother being kicked out? She had her own apartment, she cooked for herself (not the food that Pauline would like her to eat — so many prepackaged or convenience foods, tinned fruit cocktail, frozen waffles, sticky-buns — but still), she had her hair done and her clothes dry cleaned. Pauline was always very impressed with how very organized her mother, well past the allotted three score years and ten, really was.

''They sent me a letter and they are coming to see me next week. I expect they want to give me a lecture on personality and it's probably needed. But I'm ninety-two years old and I don't want to listen to it.''

At this, Pauline felt a great rush of affection for her
mother, this tiny, scrappy, dreadful woman who had,
after all, given her the gift of life. At the same time she
wondered what was the Life Expectancy in China, in
Iran, in a person with HIV virus. Her mother had lived a
long, long time. She would never be happy and she would
no doubt go to her grave, or her furnace, if she didn't
change her mind again, thinking life had somehow given
her the short end of the stick. Still, she didn't need to go
to a "Home" (what a misnomer!); she didn't deserve
that.

"Okay Mother, I'll come up with something."

"What can you do way out there on the Coast?"

"A lot. You'd be surprised. I'll fly back if necessary,
I'll —" But her mother had hung up.

Pauline stared at the telephone receiver. She was surprised to find the cord still intact. She sighed and looked
up her mother's number again and began to dial. It did
not occur to Pauline as the phone rang and rang in her
mother's apartment (she was obviously not going to
answer) that it was rather strange, after twenty years, that
she still hadn't memorized her mother's number.

The
Wild Blue
Yonder

The
Wild Blue
Yonder

"Well, that's one thing," said my father, more to himself than to me, "I won't drown."

"What do you mean, you won't drown," I asked, "why not?" We were standing at the middle of the Front Street bridge, leaning over the concrete rail, staring down into the khaki-coloured water swollen from the spring run-offs, and sharing the last of a fifteen-cent bag of Spanish peanuts. "Dawdling," as my mother would say. A trip downtown or "overtown," as the people who had been born here said, with my father was a very different thing than a trip downtown with my mother. My mother walked fast and carried a list, organized in such a way that there was never any backtracking. The shopping was done with an almost military precision, each item ticked off with a gold pencil which had been my grandfather's wedding present to my dead grandmother. It was solid gold and had come from Tiffany's in New York City. It retracted into a small golden cylinder which my mother wore on a chain around her neck. Fully open it looked like a miniature hypodermic needle made of gold. It belongs to me now, and I keep it in a little box with some other mementoes. It is not for serious writing and I have never been able to find leads that fit it properly. I never saw my mother write a letter with it, but she found it handy when she went shopping. At the end of such expeditions we had lunch in the tea-room of MacLean's Department Store where I always ordered the same thing — a peanut butter sandwich, a dill pickle and a glass of chocolate milk. Not very different from what I might have had at home. Nothing on the menu at MacLean's was very different from what one might have had at home. Eating lunch there was merely an excuse to sit down and rest a while. I always wanted to sit on a stool at the counter, but unless the room was very crowded we invariably sat in a booth. What I remember now is women with hats, their gloves and purses on the table where they could keep an eye on them, parcels stacked on the padded seats and a smell of perfumes and face powders. My mother always left a ten-cent tip because she had once been a Miss Standfast and had gone to school with the MacLean girls. She did not believe in tipping anywhere else.

My father, on the other hand. Well, my father was a dawdler, a talker, a man of impulse. A trip downtown with my father was like a mystery tour. Something would catch his eye or he would have seen a small item in the newspaper, about an auction or an exhibition or a sale of barrels at the old Cooperage. I never knew where we might end up, except that at a few minutes before 2 P.M., on a Saturday afternoon, we were handing over our money to the cashier at the Strand or the Capital or the Riviera and being ushered in to the expectant darkness which preceded the Saturday matinee. Afterwards we sometimes went to the Olympia Tea Room, run by a Greek, and shared an enormous ice-cream sundae. Models of the delights within were displayed in the front window: banana splits on glass dishes, butterscotch sundaes with cherries on top, chocolate fudge with tiny red or green parasols. When we had finished, the proprietor sometimes sat down with us and offered my father a pungent cigarette, "if the young lady doesn't object." I never objected, although my mother did when we got home and my clothes and hair still stank of cigarette smoke. Usually my father smoked Luckies and all three of us listened faithfully to the Lucky Strike Hit Parade. The big boys in grade six said L S M F T didn't stand for "Lucky Strike Means Fine Tobacco" but "Loose Sweaters Mean Floppy Tits."

But today we hadn't stopped in at the Olympia because my mother was at home preparing a special dinner. My father was on leave from his naval training base in Pensacola and tonight was his last night. Tomorrow we would see him off at the station and soon he would be on an aircraft carrier somewhere in the Pacific. It was 1942, and the movie we had just seen was "The Road to Morocco" with Bob Hope, Bing Crosby and Dorothy Lamour. We loved the "Road" movies although my mother didn't think they were really suitable for a child my age. She liked listening to Bing on records or on the radio and she agreed that Bob was doing wonders for our boys overseas but she thought the "Road" movies were vulgar.

"But how do you *know*," my father would say, laughing at some silly, remembered joke. "You've never seen one."

"All I have to do is listen to you two," she said.

I hoped, now, that the war would be over quick so that my father would be back to take me next year, when the next one came out. I wasn't to know that the war wouldn't be over quick or that the next "Road" movie wouldn't appear until 1946. Nor that the father who went away was not the father who would come back.

"What do you mean, you *can't*?" I said. "Anybody can drown."

"Not me," he said. He licked his finger and stuck it in

the bag to get the last of the salt and peanut skins; "I was born with a caul on my head."

"What's a *cawl*?" I said, with interest, thinking, from the sound of it, that it must be some kind of cape with magic feathers. Imagine knowing for sure that you couldn't drown. You would not have to wait for half an hour after you ate a picnic lunch; you could stay in the water after your lips turned blue and your teeth were tapping uncontrollably against one another; you could swim far out into a lake — an ocean even — and know that you could get back safely; you could scare your teachers and friends who would be standing on the shore with cupped hands and megaphones calling, "Come back, Frances, come back!" My father was a wonderful swimmer but he had never mentioned this *cawl* thing before.

"Well you know the baby is in a membrane, a little sac full of fluid, before she's born." I nodded, as if I had known this before, but he sensed that this was news to me and hesitated, then went on. "Remember the goldfish we won at the State Fair? You brought it home in a bag full of water, didn't you? It's rather like that. And you've seen the membrane inside an eggshell. Well, in Belfast, where I was born, it's considered very lucky to be born with a bit of that membrane stuck to the top of your head. That's called a caul. It means you can't drown. My mother said the midwife sold it to a sailor for five pounds — a lot of money for a sailor."

"But if she *sold* it," I said, staring down into the muddy waters of the Chenango, "are you still lucky?"

"Oh yes," said my father, in such a positive way that I believed him instantly.

"Is that why you joined the navy?"

"Of course." He pulled on my right pigtail. "And now, Miss Dip the Dyer's Daughter, we'd best be getting home before your mother starts to worry." We held hands as I skipped along by his side.

"Like Webster's Dictionary," we sang, "we're Morocco bound!"

"Miss Dip the Dyer's Daughter" was one of my father's pet nicknames for me. When I was in grades two and three the boys, if I wasn't careful, used to sneak up to the desk behind where I was sitting and dip my braids in the inkwell. And because we had an old pack of Happy Families that I had been given one year as a Christmas present, a pack which contained, among others, Mr Dip the Dyer and his wife and son and daughter, my father had taken to calling me "Miss Dip." He also had a card given to him by a tailor years before, which said:

I dye to live while others live to die. Your dye-ing friend —

Anton Hasenpflug

He was fond of puns and silly jokes and games of all kinds. "Happy Families" was for "three players or more" so we had to be very nice to my mother, who was not a great games player, in order to play that one. We played it the night before he left, at my request. We used pennies from my penny collection as counters although my mother worried that this might lead to a life of gambling.

I'm sure you've played this game — the player to the left of the dealer begins and asks any player for a card he or she needs to make up a family. If the player asked possesses the requested card he must give it to the asker; if not — if he hasn't got the card — he must reply, "Not at home." The turn then passes to the player who said, "Not at home."

We sat on the carpet in the sitting-room and played three or four games and then I went to bed. My father came in and sat on the edge of my bed. He took my hand from where it lay on the blanket, picked it up, turned it over and kissed the palm. Then he folded my fingers over the kiss and left. Later on, nearly asleep, I could hear my father and mother at the piano, she playing and he singing. We had stopped to buy the sheet music after we came out of the movie. "Moonlight becomes you / It goes with your hair."

Except for the tense goodbyes the next morning at the station I did not see my father again for three and a half years and for one of those years he was missing and presumed drowned.

"But he can't be drowned," I cried to my mother, when she sat me down to tell me. "He can't drown, he said so himself, he was born with a caul on his head!"

"Frances," said my grandfather, who was also there when I got home from school that afternoon, "you're a big girl now. You must learn to face things."

"But he *can't drown*," I said, hysterical with conviction, "you don't understand. He isn't dead."

"Please," said my mother, "oh please." I was led upstairs by my grandfather and told to stay in my room until I had calmed down. But I didn't calm down. I kicked at the door and screamed and called them stupid idiots until finally the doctor was called and I was given something to make me go to sleep. My father called our family doctor Mr Dose the Doctor, from the Happy Families game. Thinking of that made me start crying all over again, but I put my pillow over my face so the grown-ups wouldn't hear.

"Life must go on, I forget just why." That's the only line I can remember of a poem I had to memorize, years later, in high school. I think it begins, "Listen children, your father is dead," but I'm not really sure. Life did go on, of course. My mother took a job in the Marine Midland Bank and began a habit which was to last the rest of her life — one cigarette, and one only, after supper and after the dishes were dried and put away. She did not wear black nor did she hang a flag with a gold star in the window. My father was not officially dead, after all, although something in her manner convinced me that from that very first day she had accepted as fact that he was. It is not that my mother didn't love my father — she did. But she was a quiet, reserved woman (a "Miss Standfast" after all) and I think my father disturbed her — the way he would talk to anyone at all, the way he would suddenly break into a little soft-shoe shuffle as the three of us walked home from my grandfather's on a Sunday afternoon. Once, at an evening movie — I think it was *This Is the Army*, a musical at any rate — I saw my father put his hand on my mother's breast. "Don't *do* that," she whispered, embarrassed and angry. "Please." I always wanted to ask her, after I was grown up, why she had married him but I could never bring myself to do it. Even as a small child, a girl child, I could feel the intensity of his charm. And he had knocked about, come all the way from Ireland by himself as a teenager, read every book he could get his hands on, loved to dance, to sing, to attend parades and circuses (but not church), to play board-games and card-games (but not bridge). Oil and vinegar: neither makes a good dressing on its own, however pure the oil, however fine the vinegar. But together, in the right proportions, a perfect vinaigrette. I suppose this analogy comes to mind because every Sunday we ate dinner at my grandfather's house and I watched my grandfather mix up, in a silver tablespoon, just enough oil and vinegar, each poured from a crystal cruet, for his own personal salad of iceberg lettuce. The rest of us could do as we liked — he had his ritual and no one must criticize or challenge it.

In 1934, on his way to Albany, where he had an interview for a job, my father stopped for the day in our town. He said that he just felt a "terrible urge" to get off the train and spend a day walking around. He was leaning up against a schoolyard fence, watching a fellow demonstrate the yo-yo, and kibitzing in a friendly sort of way.

"Hey friend, show them 'The Man on the Flying Trapeze.' If they keep playing they're going to break strings and that will be more money in your pocket."

And just at that moment my mother, walking home from her part-time job at the library, turned her ankle on a broken piece of sidewalk. "Just like in the movies," my father said to me.

One of the books that was given to me just after my father went missing was *Raggedy Ann's Adventure* and a Raggedy Ann doll. I hated that book with its pious stories, and because I was still in an hysterical state inside although the outward manifestations had stopped, everything bad that happened to Raggedy Ann reminded me of the possible fate of my father. When Marcella said, "Why Raggedy Ann, you are all sticky! I do believe you are covered with jam!" I saw my father's face covered in blood. When Raggedy Ann is tied to the end of a kite and then tumbles out of the sky I saw my father falling faster and faster towards the sea. (But he couldn't drown, he told me so himself. A small voice said, 'He could die of thirst, he could starve, sharks could get him.') When the dogs are playing with her and Raggedy Ann falls into the river I saw my father floating along, his clothes sodden, praying to be rescued. Through it all Raggedy Ann keeps smiling smiling smiling. In those days Raggedy Ann dolls came with a little celluloid heart sewn inside. The heart said "I love you" and was there to represent the candy heart sewn into Raggedy Ann by the mother of the painter who drops her in the paint bucket.

I took my mother's sewing scissors and cut the heart out. I told my mother, when she scolded me, that I wanted to send the heart to Daddy, as soon as we knew where he was, but the truth was I wanted to hurt Raggedy Ann. I wanted to wipe that stupid smile off her stupid face.

My mother was older than my father, not by a lot — three years — but enough to make her embarrassed about it; she didn't like to tell her age. She had gone to New York City in her mid-twenties, to attend Katherine Gibbs Secretarial School and live with her maternal grandparents in Brooklyn. Just as she settled in with a nice job at an importer-exporter my grandmother had her first heart attack. My mother came home at once and never went back to New York. I wonder now if maybe she hadn't liked New York after all and had been glad of a legitimate excuse to come home and keep house for her parents. The only happy stories she ever told me about New York went back to her childhood and her annual visits to her grandparents. The one I liked best was about riding a streetcar with her grandma and a Chinaman got on. He put his nickel in his ear and made the conductor take it out.

My father had lived in New York and liked it — perhaps that was part of the initial attraction, his sense of adventure, his belief that anything was possible and everything was interesting. And my mother had been living at home for nine years, seven while my grandmother was alive and two after that, working at the library, keeping house for my grandfather who was head of a department at IBM. I had a little sign that said *THINK*, which he had given me to put up above my desk.

My grandmother had delivered dead baby after dead baby. Finally she had my uncle who now lived far away in Worcester, Massachusetts, and then my mother and then the doctor told my grandfather there must be no more children. When we went to put flowers on my grandmother's grave I would make daisy chains for all the little marble lambs who represented the dead babies. They had not weathered well and they looked more like drowned kittens than little lambs. Only one had a name, "Baby Louise." She had lived three months and then died of pneumonia. I wonder now if it was all those little lambs that made my mother take my father's hand from off her breast. I used to beg for a brother or sister. My mother said, "We'll see," and my father would give her a strange smile. Later she said, "It wouldn't be fair to bring a child into a world at war," and later still she didn't have to say anything — my father was Missing in Action. We had two little English girls in my class at school, evacuated from London and living with a rich but childless couple on Riverside Drive. I asked them if they'd ever been to Ireland. "The Irish are wicked," said the one called Sophie, "they won't fight in the war and they are helping the Axis."

I was horrified — was this true, that the Irish refused to fight in the war? I raced home after school and waited impatiently for my mother. If we lived over in Ireland would my father still be home? I was torn between anger — if we were in Ireland my father wouldn't be Missing in Action — and humiliation — "the Irish are wicked and they are helping the Axis."

"Southern Ireland," said my mother, unpinning her navy straw with the polka-dot veil, "Catholic Ireland. Your father's family is from Belfast." She showed me on the globe my father had bought me before he left. "Anyway," she said, "your father is an American citizen and America is at war." She said "is," not "was." It had been nine months. Did she too still believe he wasn't dead?

"Only the *Southern* Irish refuse to fight," I said to the English girls next day. "The Northern Irish, where my father comes from, they're fighting just as hard as everybody else." When it was my turn to be captain of a bat-ball team that afternoon I deliberately ignored them both, even though we had been told by our teacher to be especially nice to our new little friends from England.

About a week after this I came down with measles and my mother stayed home from her job to nurse me. We cut out paper-dolls and she read to me and let me lie and listen to the soap operas in my darkened room. And one afternoon I heard her singing, singing gaily — not a sad song but something happy and full of zip. It's strange that I can't remember what song it was but I can still remember the sound floating up to me and I realized that my mother was actually happy — that she seemed happier now than she ever had been when my father was around — that she was, in fact, quite content to have him Missing in Action and Presumed Drowned. I was filled with a terrible, helpless rage. She didn't care if he never came home again.

I know exactly when I stopped loving my mother. Nothing she could ever say later would erase that memory of the quiet afternoon in the autumn of 1945 when I lay in bed with my eyes closed and the shades pulled down and listened to the sound of my mother's singing.

("But I *knew*," she said years later, "I already knew he was alive. The War Department had sent me a message through your grandfather. He had escaped from the prison camp. I knew he'd find his way back."

"Why didn't you tell *me*! You knew how *I* felt."

"They asked me to tell no-one, until they knew exactly where he was, that he really was safe."

"I wasn't *no-one*. I could have kept a secret."

"Oh yes. Miss Blabbermouth."

"I don't believe you," I said. "I don't think you knew, then, at all." I turned away and then turned back. "If it's true, show me the telegram."

"It was a verbal message."

"I don't believe you," I said again. "You were happy he was dead.")

My mother was divorcing my father; he moved out the month before. He had agreed to give her grounds, whatever that meant. I wanted to ask someone but was sure, somehow, that the answer would be shameful. "Grounds" sounded like coffee-grounds or ground glass — something you threw out or something that could hurt you. Finally I got up the nerve to consult the big

dictionary in the public library. The entry was long and
I'm not sure how much the wiser I was, then, after I read
it. My father was going to give my mother a reason or
reasons, a motive, for the divorce. How humiliating all
this must have been for both of them, my still-gallant
father, my proper mother who could have been a brave
and cheerful widow and yet could not accept her husband
as he was now, risen from the dead — and strange.

He came back in the spring of 1946, the war in the
Pacific not yet over but over for him, at least technically,
officially. His hair had turned white and he had been
blinded in one eye. Strangely enough, what had happened
to Raggedy Ann in her kite-flying adventure had been
more or less the same as what happened to my father —
they both ended up tangled in the branches of a tree.
Only Raggedy Ann was saved by the good auspices of a
pair of robins while my father was "saved" by the
Japanese and put into a prisoner-of-war camp from which
he ultimately made his escape into the jungle. That first
night home he took my hand and said, "Frances, I really
can't talk about it yet, maybe never, is that okay? Do you
understand?"

I nodded and he began to weep, holding on to me with
one hand, my mother with the other.

"Go to bed now, Frances," said my mother.

The cake I had baked for him from an angel-food mix
stood uncut on the dining-room table. I had decorated it
with bitter chocolate icing and the heart I had cut out of
the Raggedy Ann and saved. It said, "I love you."

"What about the cake?" I said.

"Tomorrow," my mother said, and my father gave my
hand an extra hard squeeze.

"I'll put it in the cake-tin," I said, trying to keep my
voice level, "it will be just as good tomorrow."

It was agreed that my mother would keep her job at the
bank, at least for the time being, at least until my father
was on his feet again. And so it was my father who waited

at home for me every afternoon and who was the first to hear my daily adventures. Something had happened to his insides while he was overseas and he found it hard to eat anything much but what he called "nursery food": soft-boiled or scrambled eggs, junket, tapioca pudding, milk toast. Two or three times a week my mother took to eating at my grandfather's (he had an excellent cook from Georgia), ostensibly to keep her father company but no doubt so that she could eat a "proper" dinner without feeling guilty. I didn't mind eating nursery food with my father, especially as he could also eat ice-cream. He taught me a wonderful dessert, called a "Knickerbocker Glory," which was made up of cubes of red jello and green jello layered with vanilla ice-cream. After the war was over, he said we would have whipped cream with a cherry on the top, or I would, his poor excuse for a stomach perhaps no longer able to deal with the richness of whipped cream. We worked together on our Victory Garden at the bottom of Johnson Avenue. Other people, working their patches of garden — what my father called their "allotments" — greeted us warmly. My father had been "over there"; he had been shot down; he had been in a prisoner-of-war camp. He had the Congressional Medal of Honor.

"How many Japs did your father kill," the boys at school wanted to know. "Did he bring back any souvenirs?"

My father slept in the spare room because he had trouble sleeping. On Saturday mornings I sometimes crawled in with him until my mother put a stop to it. She said I was now too big for that sort of thing. It seemed to me that if somebody was having trouble sleeping you didn't shove him away in the spare room by himself; you put your arms around him and gave him a good cuddle, rubbed his back, said hush hush it's all right, I'm here, go back to sleep.

And then, after he'd been home about two months,

gradually moving around the block, then the neighbourhood, and then overtown and back, he announced one
evening to my mother and me that he'd taken a job as a
Mr Peanut for the Planters' Peanut outlet on Court
Street.

My mother stared at him. "You what?"

"I've got a job. Not a very strenuous job and not a very
well-paying job, but a job nevertheless. Ten o'clock to
two o'clock Monday to Friday, ten to five on Saturdays.
Every hour I get a fifteen-minute break."

"Mr. Peanut!" my mother put down her book. "Do
you mean to tell me you are going to dress up as Mr
Peanut and stand outside that store all day long?"

My father gave her a funny look. "Don't worry,
nobody will recognize me."

"And what do I say when they ask me how my husband is getting along?"

"You tell them he's getting along fine. You tell them
he's out and about or whatever you please. I thought
you'd *like* it that I felt well enough to take a job. And Mr
Peanut is harmless, he gives out little samples of nuts,
he's elegant, he —"

"What about the Saturday matinees?" I said. We
hadn't been since he got back, but last week he had said,
"Soon."

"This is only a temporary job," my father said. "If a
'Road' show comes to town I'll arrange a substitute."

My mother was still staring at him.

"Have you got your costume here?" I said.

"No, too precious. I have to put it on at the shop and
take it off at the shop. I start tomorrow." He turned to
my mother, who was sitting to his "good" side, and gave
her a brave defiant smile. "Come and get a free sample
when you're on your lunch-hour tomorrow. I believe it's
broken cashews."

"Frances," my mother said, "kiss your father and go
to bed."

I don't think my mother was a snob, exactly. If you are born to a certain "station" in life, as my grandparents might have said, you don't need to be a snob. And she had, after all, defied her father in order to marry a mad Irishman of no fixed address. But she was, at heart, a Standfast, and the bank she worked in was in the Standfast Block, owned by her uncle Fred. For her husband to come home from the war and take a job as a Mr Peanut must have seemed, to her, a deliberate flouting of everything she believed in. It was frivolous. And he would be standing out on the street just a few doors down from where she sat behind her beautiful oak desk, serene and smiling, dealing with Customer Accounts.

"And how is your husband getting on Mrs Grogan?"

"Better every day, thank you, Mr Kennedy."

I knew from a telephone conversation I overheard that my mother's plan had been that he would be taken on at the bank once he was really well again. He had a talent for figures and he would be given some sort of work where he could sit down most of the time and not strain his remaining eye. Now here he was, planning to be a Mr Peanut. We had been to see "Random Harvest," while he was away. Perhaps she told people my father was suffering from shell-shock, like Ronald Coleman.

Or perhaps she said nothing, hoping she knew him better than he knew himself, knowing it couldn't last.

The first week of his new job my father was in high spirits. Looking back now, I wonder if it had something to do with the fact that the very thing that affronted my mother (it could be any old Tom, Dick or Harry inside that get-up) brought a kind of relief to him. He was not James Grogan, husband of that Standfast girl, war hero, blind in one eye, recovering nicely thank you. The costume was camouflage in a bizarre sort of way — it involved a loss of identity. He was just one of dozens of Mr Peanuts; he was just a symbol.

And on the positive side, he was always a bit of a

showman. Have I told you that he was a yo-yo champion? He could do all the best tricks — Spank the Baby [Poke Him in the Tummy], Walk the Dog, the Sleeper, Around the World, even Over the Falls. To the boys and girls in my primary school he was a hero long before he ever went to war. Both he and I owned purple "diamond-studded jewelled satellites." Strange to think that the yo-yo was originally a weapon.

The peanut costume consisted of a papier-mâché peanut in the shell, open at the bottom, two armholes towards the top and small eye- and nose-holes for the face. There is a mouth, of course, sculpted on the face. It is smiling and the lips are closed. There is also a black papier-mâché top hat and a simulated snakeskin-covered cane. The rest of the outfit consists of black shirt and tights, white gloves, white spats, black shoes and a monocle on a string. When I came down with my friends on Friday afternoon he gave us all free samples of Spanish peanuts and then struck the famous Peanut pose — right arm akimbo, left foot cocked over the right, toe pointed down, the cane in his left hand planted firmly but jauntily at his side. We all applauded wildly.

That night at dinner my father seemed to have regained an almost-normal appetite. I had hung around the shop until it was time for him to quit and then we had walked up to the Home Dairy and bought various cold cuts and potato salad in a white paper box. Even squares of marble cake, although both my mother and I were excellent cake-makers.

"To be Mr Peanut," said my father, as the three of us lingered at the dining-room table, "is to be almost totally without a care in the world. To be Mr Peanut is to be blessed with a graceful and aesthetically pleasing shape; it is to wear a costume at once elegant and comfortable and suitable for any company or occasion. To be Mr Peanut is to promise only pleasure and satisfaction by the ingestion of the universally healthful nutritious and versatile goober. Who would not take comfort and inspiration in presenting such an image to the world?''

Even my mother had to smile. She took out her one cigarette of the day (she smoked Pall Malls, not Luckies) and tapped it on the table. ''Would you give me a light please, darling?''

I hugged that ''darling'' to me as I fell asleep. It was going to be all right after all.

Then Hiroshima and Nagasaki, and my father, unsmiling, his face a kind of mask, quit the Mr Peanut job and got a job as an orderly at the State Mental Hospital. ''The whole world's mad,'' he said. ''I think I'd like to go and walk amongst the harmless mad and try to cheer them up.''

''I don't want you to work at that place,'' my mother said.

''Why ever not?''

I could see her searching for a good reason. ''You aren't strong enough; you'll be on your feet all day, you'll be lifting people, you'll . . .'' she shuddered.

''I was on my feet all day in the jungle,'' my father said softly, ''all day and all night. I didn't dare go to sleep. I'm strong. And I would like to *help* somebody — I would like to feel I was of some use in this dreadful world.''

''You helped America win the war!''

''Oh yes,'' he said, ''that.''

He was a ''relief,'' which meant he worked different wards and different shifts, seven to three-thirty, three-thirty to midnight or midnight to eight. He wore white trousers, a short-sleeved white shirt, white socks, black shoes. And a great ring of keys fastened to his belt. My father had never learned to drive, so although we now had my grandfather's old La Salle, he took a bus downtown and transferred to another bus that would take him out to ''The Hill,'' which was what the people in our town called the mental hospital, when they referred to it at all. When the cool weather came he wore his greatcoat, which was now much too big for him.

My mother refused to wash his hospital clothes — she said they stank (and they did, especially when he'd been on the geriatric ward), so he washed them himself, on the weekends.

He always wangled Saturday afternoons off, so that he and I could go to the movies together. We didn't really care what we saw — it was just an excuse to be together in that warm darkness. To be together and yet not have to say much. We agreed that *The Road to Utopia* wasn't as good as the earlier "Road" shows but it was still pretty funny. I did not ask what it was like working on The Hill, nor did he volunteer any information. He and my mother were barely speaking. People from the west side of the city (our side) did not work on The Hill, unless they were the surgeons, who volunteered a certain number of hours a month, or men of the cloth. People from the east side of the city worked there — Hungarians, Ukrainians, Italians, bog Irish. I was never allowed to go over to the east side of the city, although I knew my father had often been over there, before the war, because he liked to go everywhere and loved the walk. The east side of the city was full of people with strange-sounding names: Koneckney, Gretsky, Rasmussen, Konowalyk. When my father moved out, to give my mother grounds for divorce, he took a room in the house of one of the staff nurses, Mrs Grabowski, whose son played outfielder for the Triplets. I began to learn about baseball.

On my eleventh birthday my mother gave me a lovely birthday party to which my father was not invited. No one said anything, for the fathers were often absent from children's birthday parties. The next day, after church and dinner at my grandfather's, my father took me out for a long walk. We ended up on the bridge, leaning over the railing.

"I love her," he said. "She doesn't believe it, but it's

true. But I can't fit in.'' He held my hand tight. "You must never never think you have to choose between us.'' Then he gave me my present, an album of Bing Crosby songs.

"Will you spend Christmas with us?'' I asked.

"I'll try. But I might have to work that day.''

I nodded.

"You know,'' he said to the river, "if I hadn't been shot down and been in that dreadful camp, I would have deserted. I think,'' he said bitterly, "that this will be the last war where young men will line up to enlist. Eighteen-year-olds! Nineteen-year-olds! Terrible.'' He looked at me and laughed a pain-filled laugh. "It's too wild up there in the wild blue yonder.''

By Christmas he was dead. The man who could not drown died, in the end, by water. He had volunteered for relief duty on the Violent Ward and was working midnight to eight when some of the patients ganged up on him and the Practical Nurse, tied them up, turned the fire hose on them, and forced all those tons of water down their throats.

It shouldn't have happened; even in the days before Thorazine there were ways of controlling extreme and violent patients — strait jackets, locked rooms, barbiturates, paraldehyde. Something went terribly wrong and there was an official investigation. My father had not been allowed to give medication, nor had the PN. Something went wrong on the previous shift but the record book said that all the appropriate medication and procedures had been given out or followed. Books can be falsified however and Mrs Grabowski, who testified at the hearing, said that it was a known fact that many of the nurses kept the more "interesting'' drugs (her word, not mine) for themselves. The whole thing was reported in both the *Sun* and the *Press*. It was a scandal, they said.

GOVERNOR DEWEY DEMANDS
COMPLETE INVESTIGATION.

My mother was granted a leave of absence from the bank and she took me out of school. She and my grandfather and I went on a trip to Saranac Lake, where I discovered that my mother, who hated sports, was an excellent ice-skater, much much better than I, who had weak and wobbly ankles. My grandfather signed the register Mr William Standfast and Family. My mother, over the bridge table, let it be inferred that her husband had died in the War.

We skated together, my grandfather in a long, black wool coat with a velvet collar and my mother, also in black, with me between them in last year's leggings and Sunday coat. My grandfather held my left hand, my mother my right. We stared straight ahead as we moved down the ice and the other people at the resort called out, "My, don't you make a picture!" The tears froze on my cheeks.

I still have my father's letters, the ones he wrote specifically to me. Just before he went missing he sent me a letter which ended with that famous line of Mabel, the Talking Camel: "This is the screwiest picture I ever was in." Somehow I derived great comfort from that remark. I still do.

Also available from Penguin Books

Audrey Thomas

GOODBYE HAROLD, GOOD LUCK

These thirteen stories, introduced by the author, make up a refreshing collection ranging in style from stark realism to delicious fantasy. They are all vivid, moving stories, whether reflecting the subtle nuances of contemporary sexual relationships or the strong link between mother and daughter. Several are fascinating and playful approaches to language; others are powerful evocations of atmosphere and place.

This collection confirms Audrey Thomas's reputation as a brilliant writer of short stories, and as a compassionate observer of the rich landscape of human emotions.

"Thomas has a faultless ear for dialogue, for how people sound... and she has a camera eye for detail."

Margaret Atwood

"A splendid and thoroughly engaging piece of writing....Her touch with short fiction is nothing short of dazzling."

Vancouver Sun

"Thomas's stories do bloom, with all the trumpeted magnificence, sometimes, of an amaryllis bulb, or, at other times, with the scratchy nostalgia of an old song played on an antique gramophone."

Kingston Whig-Standard

Alice Munro

THE PROGRESS OF LOVE

Winner of the Governor General's Award

With all the ease and mastery that have won extraordinary international acclaim for her writing, the eleven stories in this collection by Alice Munro invite us into the most intimate moments of human experience — moments of realization about the power, the tenderness and the sacrifice of love.

"Alice Munro richly deserves recognition as one of the foremost contemporary practitioners of the short story."
The New York Times

"Moments of insight flash from the pages like lightning."
Philadelphia Enquirer

"Munro's understanding of family life is intricate and profound ....*The Progress of Love* is marvellous."
The Toronto Star

"Alice Munro has earned glowing testimonials for her previous collections of short stories and *The Progress of Love* will bring her many more of them. She deserves them all."

The London Evening Standard

"One of the year's 10 best fiction books."
The New York Times Book Review, 1986

Mordecai Richler

THE STREET

"On St. Urbain Street, a head start was all. Our mothers read us stories from *Life* about pimply astigmatic fourteen-year-olds who had already graduated from Harvard....We were not supposed to memorize baseball batting averages or dirty limericks....If we didn't make doctors, we were supposed to at least squeeze into dentistry."

Here is Mordecai Richler at his hilarious best in these lively stories inspired by his own childhood. The time is the 1940s, and the place is Montreal's St. Urbain Street. On the street, Tansky's Cigar & Soda is a home for its argumentative "regulars," secret copies of *The Art of Kissing* are furtively consulted, and the resident Jews eye the nearby French Canadians with suspicion.

And on the street the famous Duddy Kravitz proffers sexual advice (which is much needed because Richler's mother had told him that babies come from department stores and had threatened to exchange him for a girl).

It all ads up to a feast of wit and nostalgia from the acclaimed author of *The Apprenticeship of Duddy Kravitz, Joshua Then and Now* and *Solomon Gursky Was Here.*

"A marvellous writer and one of immense cleverness besides."

Kingston Whig-Standard

"Unclassifiable, inimitable and — excellent."

Al Purdy, *Canadian Literature*